DOUBLE TROUBLE

A Magical Romantic Comedy (with a body count)

RJ BLAIN

DOUBLE TROUBLE
A MAGICAL ROMANTIC COMEDY (WITH A BODY COUNT)
BY RJ BLAIN

Layla, a recovering drug addict, reformed kleptomaniac, and general troublemaker, believes she has a one-way ticket straight to hell to go with her general rap sheet. Instead of jail time, she's ordered to perform ninety days of community service.

Her job is simple: she must keep two unicorns out of trouble.

It doesn't take her long to learn the truth: she's been assigned to a dose of double trouble, and wherever the unicorns go, chaos and mayhem follow in their wake.

One wants to take over the world.

The other wants in her pants.

Unless she pulls out all the stops, Layla won't escape her community service time single or sane.

Warning: this novel contains magic, mayhem, unicorns, romance, and bodies. Proceed with Caution.

Cover design by Daqri Bernardo of Covers by Combs.

ONE

Why couldn't I have been born a
good girl?

IN ALL MY time touring North Carolina's judiciary system, the judge leading a pair of
white unicorns into the courtroom took the
cake. Damned cupcakes. If it hadn't been for
some damned pixie-dust laced cupcakes a
few months ago, I might've stayed out of jail
for a change, but no. Someone had left pixie-
dust infused cupcakes sitting out where I
could grab them. Pixie dust beat the other
crap I'd shot up, ingested, or otherwise taken
during my days as a druggy.

I'd gone down on those cupcakes with my
typical kleptomaniac's restraint, but I hadn't
even gotten to eat one before I'd gotten
busted for possession. The count of possession landed me in the slammer for thirty
days. The icing on top of the cake that was
my life?

My judge had two unicorns with him,

which meant I dealt with someone crazier than me. Why couldn't I have been born a good girl? I'd escaped my mother's womb destined to create trouble. I'd been so troublesome that I'd landed right into the system, as love sure as hell couldn't conquer all, and my mother had presented my father with two choices: get rid of me or drown me in the nearest river.

My mother had won that war, but my father sent a card on my birthday every year. Enough to let me know he still cared—but not enough to risk my mother's love. Go figure.

If I could've stolen anything I wanted, I would've taken dear old dad just to stick it to my asshole mother, who wanted a bed of roses and a perfect child. She'd gotten me instead, and she liked claiming maybe I was the devil's daughter rather than some Egyptian chick with cat-like tendencies.

I'd love to be an Egyptian chick with cat-like tendencies.

Then, since my problems obviously had room to worsen, an angel popped into existence near the witness stand.

Great. I'd graduated from a menace to the general public to requiring the state to request divine intervention to deal with me.

The angel's laughter silenced the typical courtroom chatter. My attorney, an esquire so new the ink hadn't fully dried on her law license, grunted. Someone needed to tell her grunting made her sound rather like a cow giving birth.

My last community service tour had dumped me on a cow farm, as the judge thought I'd been so full of bullshit I'd be best off learning how to be a productive member of society from my kin. I'd liked that man; he'd told the truth and hadn't minded when I'd guffawed at his verdict.

The unicorns flattened their ears and regarded the angel with open disdain. The angel fluttered his wings, and the golden bands on the white piqued my interest enough that I sat up for a better look.

"I'm a she today," the angel corrected, as she laughed again.

"Well, call me baby and spank me with a spork," I replied with wide eyes. "You just pick when you want to be a man angel or a woman angel at your whim?"

"That is correct. First time?"

"In jail, at court, meeting an angel, seeing a unicorn, or mouthing off to a judge?"

"I was going for meeting an angel, but I am curious to hear your answers for all." The angel hopped, landed on the banister, and made herself comfortable.

"You know, if I sat on the witness stand like that while naked, I'd be tossed into prison

again, but probably without parole this time."
I considered the unfairness of it all, although
I guess she met the basic standards of society;
she didn't have nipples or genitals of any sort.
"No, no, yes, yes, and no. I figured they'd wait
for a bigger offense than stealing some laced
cupcakes before they called in the big guns to
deal with me. That'll be a fun story to tell my
next roommate while in the slammer. I'm so
much trouble the court system required divine intervention to decide what to do
with me."

"All rise. This court is now in session with
the Honorable Judge Marlow Davids presid-
ing," the bailiff announced. I hadn't run into
him before, a surprise considering how many
times I'd been to courthouses scattered across
the state.

"All but the jury may be seated." The judge,
rather than sitting as I expected, stood behind
his chair and overlooked the crowd of curious onlookers.

For some damned reason or another, my
sessions tended to draw a crowd. I bet it was
my charming personality, my natural curls, or
that I always managed to find a way to entertain.

The rest of my life involved hopping from
prison to prison and courtroom to courtroom, so why not enjoy it? I'd done a good
enough job; I'd kicked the nasty drugs, al-

though pixie dust always managed to break my good streak. It didn't count, did it? Pixie dust, when paid for properly, was fair game. I hadn't even stolen cupcakes with the good stuff. The high might've lasted for ten minutes. Maybe.

The bailiff swore the jury in, and I muttered over my damned luck.

Why did a cupcake theft need a damned jury?

Oh, right. I'd put so many counts of theft onto my rap sheet the judges no longer printed them out for fear of breaking the tables. Given a year and a few opportunities, my list of crimes would be longer than the tax code.

After the state prosecutor and my attorney did their opening dance, the judge sat, made me sit at the witness stand, swore me in, and slapped a folder to the polished surface of his stand. He heaved a sigh. "Instead of the standard questioning session, we're going to do things a little differently today, as we have an angel in attendance to make sure the truth and nothing but the truth is spoken for this trial. I recommend against any acts of perjury, as you will be caught. Miss Kellen, what do you have to say for yourself this time?"

"I only regret I didn't get to eat one of the cupcakes before being apprehended for stealing them. It seems like a shame I get to spend the rest of my life in prison without tasting the cupcakes first. It's obvious, Your Honor. I have a kleptomaniac's restraint, and it's not like being a goody-goody will do me a lick of good at this stage." As I was rather proud of my rap sheet rivaling the tax code, I asked, "If you printed my rap sheet, would it compare to the tax code yet? I have a burning need to know. I mean, I'd definitely like to know before I accept my one-way ticket to hell. That's why you brought in an angel, right? North Carolina has finally come to terms that I'm unsalvageable and has re-quested my custody be transferred to Satan? It would be a sensible thing to do."

Everyone in the courtroom stared at me, and Judge Davids lifted his hand and rested it against his forehead, likely praying for patience.

He'd need a lot of it to deal with me. Some criminals did the whole remorse thing well, but I'd figured out from an early age I lacked any sort of redeeming quality. Why live a lie?

My attorney bowed her head. "I apologize, Your Honor."

"It's certainly not your fault that your client is difficult at best, Esquire." Judge Davids slapped the desk with the folder again. Did he really think it would help? I'd learned the hard way that smashing one's head or property into things didn't do jack shit on a good day. I assumed the judge was not having a good day.

I was involved in the case, and that would make his life difficult by default.

The angel snorted.

"How does a being without a head snort?" I asked.

"Very carefully," she replied. "The splendor of my appearance would wipe you out of existence, and I'd rather not disintegrate any curious mortals today. It's such a burden being so magnificent."

"Isn't pride a sin?"

"No. Pride without substance is a sin. I spoke nothing but the truth."

"Are all angels as badass as you are?"

"As a matter of fact, yes."

Hot damn with a hell of a good cupcake. "You must be pretty miffed you got called in to deal with a cupcake thief. I mean, if I were in charge of the judicial system, I wouldn't have fast-tracked little old me for some divine intervention. While my kleptomaniac tendencies tend to cost the system money, there's a difference between a courtroom for twenty minutes to confirm I'm unsalvageable versus an angel and a circus. No offense to the jury who was recruited, probably against their will, to take part in this circus. But this circus has *unicorns*. How cool is that? I just thought unicorns were even more of a myth than angels until now, but this circus has two unicorns. Which is pretty nuts. Shouldn't the real cases get the unicorns? Like a serial killer or something?"

"Miss Kellen," the judge scolded. "It's not social hour."

It wasn't? I scoffed at that, but I sat back in my seat and waited for the judge to get around to making me answer more questions guaranteed to send me back to prison where I belonged.

"As it has been generally determined from your record and behavior in court that traditional rehabilitation methods are unsuitable for your specific circumstances, the court has decided you will need more extreme measures to ensure you become a viable part of society rather than a menace and a drain."

"To be fair, I think I'm only a menace to myself and any pixie-dust laced products, such as cupcakes, that happen to be left unattended in my path. I haven't touched the hard stuff in six months. And let me tell you, the withdrawal off that shit is a monster. If you're looking for reassurances I won't be diving back into that crap, well, I walked by a dealer with the kind of stuff that'll put you in your grave before I spotted the cupcakes, and I managed to say no. Actually, I deserve the cupcakes for saying no to the nastier temptation. The cupcakes were too much, though. Pixie dust won't kill you. It might make you a mindless slave for a while if you get the good stuff, but it won't kill you."

I'd been pretty proud of saying no for like the first time in my life. Temptation hadn't gotten me until I'd seen the damned cupcakes. They'd been double chocolate with a pink, glittery coating on top, begging me to eat one.

They'd just looked so damned tasty.

"She speaks the truth," the angel announced. "Additional detoxification might be an idea, as she is still struggling with withdrawal and dependency issues, but she is genuinely making an effort. Had the pixie dust been delivered in a fashion other than a cupcake, she may even have resisted. I do believe the delivery method was more enticing than the drug itself."

I considered my thoughts, realized the angel made a damned good point, and shrugged. "Give me a hot man and a double chocolate cupcake. I'd eat right out of his hand and off his chest, and I'd take extra care with the crumbs and icing. He'd be very clean when I finished with him and my cupcake. It's a real issue."

The angel snickered, as did the entirety of the jury.

"Miss Kellen, please try to remember this is a court of law," the judge scolded.

"Oh, I remember. I just don't care. It's not like I didn't earn being here. If I'm going to go down, I may as well have some fun with it. Being all sober and serious isn't going to make my case look any better. I stole the cupcakes, and really, not even an angel can save me from myself. I'm a bad egg, and that's that. Just ask my mother."

"The court is of the opinion that parental abuse is the reason you're troubled, and we have sufficient evidence to warrant extenuating circumstances regarding your behavior, and that a non-traditional rehabilitation method is required. For most thieves and criminals, traditional methods can render acceptable results for reform. The system, frankly, has failed to consider your specific circumstances," Judge Davids replied. "As such, the state of North Carolina requested additional assistance with your case. There are victims, such as the owner of the cupcakes you stole, and then there are those like you."

"You mean long-term drug addicts with a kleptomaniac's restraint?"

The angel laughed. "You're rather fond of that phrase. It's cute, really."

Huh. An angel thought I was cute? "When you decide you're a male angel, how do you feel about humans eating cupcakes off your chest? I mean, you do have a very nice chest, and I currently have a selection of zero male chests for eating cupcakes from."

"While I am flattered you believe my chest is suitable for your cupcake-eating adventures, I think you will find you will be able to abandon your current innocence through the seductive use of confectionaries in the future in a much more beneficial manner," the angel replied with laughter in her voice.

I could listen to an angel laugh all day long without regret. "I should feel sad I've been rejected by an angel, but you find me amusing, and I'm all right with that. Also, you seem strangely confident I might be able to have a cupcake-eating adventure involving the chest of a man. I'd much prefer a smoking hot man, but honestly, I'll take any half-decent man available."

Virginity was overrated, but most men my age seemed to want clean, nice women to be the mother of their little babies. I had worked hard at the being clean part of things, but I had a long way to go in the nice department, and the last thing I wanted was to be a mother like my mother.

"You're a refreshing human."

"I hope that doesn't mean you're about to liquify me and drink me down like a glass of lemonade. Lemonade is refreshing. I'm not sure people juice would be refreshing, and I don't really want to find out."

The angel laughed. "You are at no risk of being liquified and treated like a glass of lemonade."

"Well, that's something. Not as good as a cupcake on a hot man, but I can work with it."

"Miss Kellen, please try not to turn this court into a circus," Judge Davids chided.

"Were you expecting anything other than a circus in a courtroom with two unicorns, an angel, and a jury likely regretting they got out of bed this morning once they realized they had to deal with me?"

"I was hoping for something other than a circus, as this is a courtroom."

"Honestly, I'm okay if we just skip straight to the sentencing. That file tells you everything you need to know about me, and I don't think even an angel could salvage anything from me at this point in time. It's not like the state of North Carolina hasn't been trying since I turned three."

"That is part of the reason there's an angel in attendance today. You have been in the foster system since you were three, and there have been little to no positive results after you were sent to correctional facilities."

"Well, yeah. What do you expect when your mother wanted to drown you in the nearest body of water because you're a menace? I can't really say it's my fault specifically. Infants are generally innocent enough creatures, and she wanted to off me since the day I was born. I mean, it's nice that Dad sends cards for my birthday, but let's not delude ourselves here. He's probably glad I'm out of the picture. Maybe he wised up and started making use of birth control since my mother's too stupid to. She would've saved herself a lot of problems if she'd bothered with base protections since she didn't want kids that badly. Dad? He actually likes helpless humans, which is probably why I survived up until the age of three to enter the system."

Silence was a funny thing. When large numbers of people crowded into small spaces, a room never fell truly silent, but the courtroom got as close as it could. A few shifted in their seats, likely uncomfortable with my blunt admissions on my upbringing —or lack thereof. Some probably considered the psychological damage of someone's mother wanting to drown them from birth.

Judge Davids stared in the general vicinity of where the angel's head should have been. "Would you verify the truth of her statement, please?"

"Humanity is both capable of the greatest of goods and the worst of sins. She spoke the truth and nothing but the truth, no matter how difficult that truth is to hear."

Great. Even the angel pitied me. I was on a roll. Maybe instead of a standard prison, they'd send me off so I could join the rest of the lunatics up for treatments in the government's system. "I don't suppose someone has a spare cupcake topped with pixie dust available? I could use one right about now."

Unless North Carolina changed its tune and removed me from its list of drug abusers, I wouldn't be seeing much of any pixie dust, as they required photo identification to place any order. Mine had a little logo that stated I wasn't to be given any substances whatsoever, including pixie dust.

"I trust you are aware that even pixie dust violates your current terms of parole, Miss Kellen?"

I shrugged. "Yep. Personally, I think it's stupid. If I could just wander to a coffee shop and walk out with a high, I probably wouldn't have experimented as hard on that crap that probably cut off a good twenty years of my life. The good girls and boys get the highs us abusers are denied. I mean, I could leave North Carolina, except I'd just start making a new rap sheet in a different state. Not that I can afford to leave North Carolina. Well, unless you brought the unicorns so I could steal one and ride off into the sunset?" I eyed the two animals, which looked like white horses with gray tinging their muzzles. "Your unicorns look a little corrupted. They're not pure white. I thought they were supposed to be pure white. Are they naughty unicorns with their naughtiness showing?" I pointed at the larger of the two, very obviously a stallion with his head held high. "That one looks particularly naughty. He has more gray than the other one. I'm not sure if the other one is a male or female, but he's definitely a male."

"The other one is a she. They are standard unicorns, and as they age, their coats will brighten. They're rather young."

"They are? How young are they?"

"The stallion is in his early thirties, and his sister is in her twenties. By fifty, they will be true white," the judge replied. "You may not steal either unicorn."

"Well, that's a pity. I think I should be able to steal one of them. You brought them here. Isn't that the equivalent to inviting me to steal one? I'm well known for stealing things. Apparently, possession being a specific fraction of the law does not actually apply."

"I didn't bring them here to be stolen, Miss Kellen."

I rolled my eyes at that. "You could compromise with me. Come on, it's just one unicorn."

"You can't steal a unicorn, but you will be accompanying both of them to a place of this court's choosing for your rehabilitation program."

My mouth dropped open, and I stared at the judge. "We already know I'm crazy, but if you need help, I can recommend a few good psychologists. North Carolina helpfully provides them for the crazy people like me, but with all due respect, Your Honor, that's just nuts."

According to the judge's expression, he gave my words some serious thought. "Miss Kellen, please."

"If you already know what you're going to do with me, why is there even a jury? I mean, trials are supposed to be about trying me for a crime, right? This is more like a disjointed circus where the ringmaster has finally snapped, the critters are staging a revolt, and the angel... well, I'm not sure why the angel is really here. I might have no restraint and a tendency to steal things, but I'm honest about it. I'm the most honest crook there is. Straighter than an arrow, that's me. Also, since we're being all forthcoming and everything, I'm definitely way straighter than an arrow. No crazy stuff for me. I guess I probably wouldn't say no if an incubus strutted up and asked me to lick a cupcake off his chest. I mean, who am I kidding? I'm definitely not saying no to that."

"Miss Kellen, please. Your love life is not up on trial."

"It wouldn't be much of a trial. My sexual misconduct record is non-existent."

"Miss Kellen."

"What? It's true. My sexual conduct record? Also, non-existent. Look, even in prison, the inmates? They don't want this sort of crazy. Actually, I have a history of shanking anyone who tries anything stupid, and I get real creative when I shank some-one," I chirped.

"Please tell me she's not telling the truth," the judge begged.

"She's telling the truth," the angel confirmed.

"Why aren't these shanking incidents listed in your record?"

"Because the prison guards reviewed the tapes and determined it was an act of self-de-fense. Self-defense in prison doesn't get added to the record. If they hadn't tried to get uppity, I wouldn't have had a need to shank them." I shrugged. "Let me tell you something, though. Shanking someone with a bowl is hard work."

Once again, silence fell over the room, and both unicorns stared at me. The stallion canted his head, one ear twisted back and one ear forward.

"Yeah, buddy. I'd wise up and put those

nice, shiny hooves of yours to good use, as I am totally the kind to shank a bitch with a bowl."

The judge looked ready to cry. "How do you shank someone with a bowl?"

"You hit them really hard, and when it finally breaks, you use the edge as your shank. You hit them really hard numerous times until you cut them. For the record, prison bowls? They don't really make good shivs or shanks. They don't like giving inmates anything that might be used as a shiv. I mean, the bowl definitely did some cutting, but it's really the wrong shape to classify as either a shiv or shank. The guards praised me for defending myself until they could intervene, however. When in prison and there's not much else to do, well, I exercise." I showed off my rather defined bicep. "See?"

As someone who rarely received praise, I'd basked in the glow of having beat an asshole with a bowl and being complemented on doing it.

"She is telling the truth," the angel confirmed.

"The jury is present to evaluate your case and determine how long is a fair time for your punishment and rehabilitation," the judge announced.

"I thought that was your job. You just go

with it if the jury says I'm guilty. By the way, I'm guilty."

"The court has decided that your situation requires special care. It's obvious our previous measures have been ineffective."

"The court, with all due respect, Your Honor, has lost its marbles providing someone like me with an angel and two unicorns. I'm still not sure how the unicorns play into this, as you seem determined to prevent me from stealing them. I'd totally steal the stallion, though. I could put him up on show and make a fortune showing him off. He's pretty. You can't show me pretty things and expect me to not want to steal them. Sorry to the unicorn's sister. You're also pretty, but he's totally prettier. He looks extra naughty with a side dish of naughty, and apparently, I like that sort of thing? You're kind of pure compared to him."

The unicorns stared at me, likely questioning why they'd agreed to become involved with my case.

"The unicorns require a caretaker, Miss Kellen. You have been selected."

A laugh burst out of me, and I doubled over, tears stinging my eyes while I gasped for breath. "You have got to be kidding me."

"He is telling the truth," the angel announced.

"Did someone finally counter shank me in

prison? This could be a concussion-induced hallucination that just happened to coincide with my court date. Let me tell you, I've been looking forward to this." I checked my non-existent watch, as inmates weren't allowed such nice things. It was less that it was a nice thing, and more that a few inmates had figured out how to weaponize even watches, so they were taken away as a safety precaution.

I had a little to do with that, as I'd taken a watch and forcibly shoved it down an ass-hole's throat for trying to cop a feel. If the asshole hadn't tried to cop a feel, I wouldn't have gotten creative.

"That gesture worries me," the judge muttered.

"Two months, three weeks, and three days waiting to meet you, Judge Davids. That's what my attorney told me earlier. Really, you seem pretty cool for a judge, so the wait was worth it." I checked my imaginary watch and squinted. "My hour and minute hands seem to have vanished, so I can't give you the exact time, sorry."

"It takes time to make arrangements of this nature. You also signed the paper consenting to a delay in your trial for your cupcake theft. You told your parole officer you deserved a minimum of three months for snatching the cupcake, and that you thought this was fair."

"Well, it is. I totally violated my parole. Honestly, I do not understand why I was let out on parole in the first place. I'm hopeless."

"The court doesn't feel that way. The court feels that you haven't been given sufficient opportunities to experience a positive household with responsibilities and rewards for accomplishing those responsibilities."

"You mean a paycheck?"

"I do."

"Inmates get a paycheck, almost. Sorta. Well, not really. It's a buck fifty an hour, and if we get through our parole terms, the state cuts the check as compensation. I mean, I assume the rest of the minimum wage went to the taxes and boarding expenses of being in jail, which is fair enough, but a buck fifty an hour doesn't go all that far, or so I've been told. As I've never made it through parole, that check's not coming. I'm just being realistic. But the motivational stubs I get once a month are fun to think about, I guess. Let's say you all let me out of parole today. According to my attorney, if I'm released on a six-month term and if I make it, I'd get a check for fifty thousand dollars. For the record, that's for fifteen years as paid work, as they kindly started paying me to do work when I was twelve. Or so my attorney says. Also, Your Honor, you should probably tell somebody child labor is bad. I'm not exactly the shining example of goodness here, but even I've figured that out."

Ah, good old silence spurred on by the discomfort of those just realizing for the first time their system really made use of child labor as part of its rehabilitation program.

The judge scowled and flipped through my file. "The judiciary system didn't see fit to include your prison work record with your general information."

"Well, it'd be real stupid of them to put in just how much they'd owe me if I ever did make it out of the slammer. Also, they don't pay out overtime, and they assume we get two weeks of vacation, which we don't. We work six days a week, eight hours a day when in the work camps, and even if we're not assigned to a work camp, we're doing *something* productive to the system. Also, if you ever tear those robes, let me know. I've got a mean stitch, and I can make those tears disappear without a trace. I'm not a great person, sure, but I work like I mean it."

I had plans for my fifty thousand if I ever got my dirty hands on it.

"Can you verify the truth of her statement, please?"

"She's telling the truth," the angel reported, and I marveled that a being lacking a head could spit words so effectively. "I would recommend you ask a few questions regarding when she first learned to sew in the prison system."

I enjoyed the angel's laughter, but her anger made me want to leave the room immediately and climb into the nearest sewer, where it'd be a lot safer.

"Thank you. Miss Kellen? How old were you when you learned to sew in the prison system?"

"How old was I when I went to prison for the first time? It's been a while."

"I have the date here. You were five, almost six."

"That old."

"She speaks the truth," the angel announced.

"How many hours were you expected to sew or do other tasks?"

"Not much has changed over the years," I replied, wondering if I stepped into some form of trap or another.

"When did you learn to read and write?"

I arched a brow at the judge. "Who said I could read or write?"

For the first time in my life, I witnessed a judge erupt, spew curses vile enough even my fellow inmates hesitated to use them, and storm out of the courtroom, informing everyone between profanities the court session would resume in an hour. He ushered in a different sort of silence, one I wanted to break before the attention of everyone in the room made me snap, too.

I shrugged. "If you think the read and write thing is bad, I count to a hundred by counting how many times it takes me to count to ten. After that, things get a little confusing, but whatever. That whole thing with fifty thousand? That's what I was told when I asked the corrections officer, which my attorney confirmed. Bless their hearts, they did try to explain the numbers to me, but they don't make sense, you know? But don't worry about it. I just ask somebody to read for me if needed. It's not a big deal, really."

If anything, my words deepened the silence.

"It is a big deal," the angel said, and all I heard was sadness in her tone. "That is the sound of guilt, for even the hardest of hearts understand you were robbed of something far more valuable than anything you have pilfered over your years."

"Huh. Really? What's that?"

"Your childhood, of course."

Of course. "Well, I'm not really worried about it. I mean, what would I even do with fifty thousand? Well, beyond buy cupcakes. Hey, how many cupcakes could I buy with that much?"

"I could tell you the number, but would it mean anything to you?" the angel asked.

"Well, not really. Is it a lot of cupcakes?"

"You could fill this entire courtroom with cupcakes with that much money."

My eyes widened, and I whistled. "I'm going to need a really patient man if I'm going to be eating that many cupcakes off his chest. Damn."

The angel laughed, and I appreciated how everyone else in the room relaxed at the sound. "And many, many long years."

I guess I would, to eat that many cupcakes. "Oh, well. A girl can dream, right?"

"You certainly can," the angel replied, her tone solemn. "But I'm certain you can find something better to do with all that money."

"You act like I'll ever see it."

"You will," the angel replied. "It's only a matter of time. I think you'll still find things will work out in your favor for a change."

"That'll take a miracle," I muttered.

"Or a pair of unicorns and a few cupcakes."

"With pixie dust on top?"

The angel laughed. "You won't need any pixie dust to find happiness. You'll see."

Angels were crazy, but since I wasn't one to talk, I kept quiet.

TWO

I'd name her Pissy, personally.

AFTER AN HOUR, Judge Davids returned, the clerk went through the motions of opening the session, and the attorneys—both of them —went under fire over my criminal record, the system, and anything else he felt had gone wrong with my so-called rehabilitation. To add a complication to my situation, the system owed me more than I'd been told, not that I understood the numbers the judge discussed with the attorneys.

My attorney argued for another court session, one that would audit my earnings while part of the prison system determined if my skills had resulted in my constant cycling through various jails rather than proper rehabilitation. One that would establish how much I would be owed following a successful rehabilitation.

The judge listened to the attorneys argue over whether or not my case should be reviewed immediately or delayed for more research. Twenty minutes into the debate, the judge snapped, "Enough. The jury will decide if this is resolved now or later, as we have an angel in attendance. Does the jury require time to discuss, or do you feel you can come to a decision with what you have heard?"

Every jury had some poor schmuck who had to speak for everyone, and after a minute of chatter, the appointed sacrifice stood and announced, "We do not need additional time to discuss, Your Honor."

I wondered if I could wander out without anyone noticing. While I sat beside my attorney, she focused on the other attorney and the judge. The angel's attention fell on me now and then, but she seemed more interested in the unicorns. The stallion kept a close watch on me, while his sister's ears flattened back, and she whipped her tufted tail.

"I'm naming the girl one Beast, and the boy one Patience. Maybe Stalker," I whispered to my attorney.

"I'd name her Pissy, personally."

Well, I'll be damned with sprinkles. My attorney had a sense of humor. "The angel got to you, didn't she?"

"This whole case has gotten to me. I have some prison system clerks to correct. With my foot. Directly up their asses. I'll line them up in order of responsibility, and the worst offenders will experience my wrath several times."

Well, that mental image would haunt me for a while. I peeked under the table, confirming my attorney wore stiletto heels. "They're going to need surgery and a lot of pixie dust to recover from that."

"Correctional officers are not allowed to indulge in pixie dust within twenty-four hours of duty, and they're scanned before shifts to make certain they aren't under the influence."

Hah. No wonder they got pissy with the rowdy inmates. "I'd always thought pixie dust was a requirement to deal with the inmates."

Judge Davids cleared his throat. "Ladies, if you're done gossiping?"

I raised my hand. "Do I get a say in this?"

"No."

"Well, that's harsh."

"What is the jury's decision?"

"The jury wishes for the information to be reviewed now while it can be verified by an angel. According to what we've been told, the correctional officer in charge of her file is present at the courthouse today, so it would be more efficient for the court to resolve this situation now."

"I'm pretty sure that's not how courts are supposed to work," I muttered to my attorney.

"It's not, but judges have a great deal of leeway in handling a case with an angel in attendance, as it's simpler to get to the heart of the matter. The approval for the use of an angel gives the judge a lot more options than during a regular trial. So, everything you've experienced in court will be quite different from this. I expect it will take no more than ten minutes to resolve."

"That's it? Just ten minutes?"

"That's it. If the correctional officer is brought in, I'll ask a few questions, the angel will verify the truth, and it'll be simple to determine if you were wrongfully incarcerated or given unfair parole terms to prevent rehabilitation."

"Like barring pixie dust after I'd been clean for six months?"

"That's a very good question, and it's one I don't have the answer to. Your Honor?"

"Ask," Judge Davids ordered.

"Considering the value of the cupcake, would the court conclude my client should be returned to prison if she did not have a flag barring pixie dust on her record?"

"Of course not," the judge replied. "The cupcake was recovered, undamaged, although it was ultimately consumed by the shop owner rather than a customer. The total charge for such a cupcake is no more than fifteen dollars."

I sighed. "I hate numbers. I have no idea if that's valuable or not."

"If you were being paid a fair wage, you would be able to afford one after an hour's worth of work."

"That's it? I could work for an hour and have a cupcake?"

"Yes, approximately. It's more complicated than that."

"Well, I figured that much out. Mostly. Somewhat." I shrugged. "Okay, really, I have no idea what you mean."

"I believe she is trying to tell you she has zero idea how money works, how it is supposed to be used, and the appropriate way to use it, and had she benefited from a proper education, she would have simply paid for the cupcake rather than steal it."

"They give me this card when I'm on parole, and I was told if I give it to people, it would work, but I didn't know who to give it to or how to use it," I admitted. "And then it was just easier to pilfer what I needed. And that would land me right back into jail."

"She is speaking the truth," the angel announced.

"Take the stand, Miss Kellen," Judge Davids ordered. "This court will judge based on your testimony."

I hopped to my feet, and on my way to the stand, I slapped the stallion's rump. He squealed, jumped and bucked, and landed with a startled snort. If I'd been any closer, he might've nailed me with his hooves, but as he hadn't hit me, I viewed myself the victor. Snickering over having goosed the stalker horse with a horn, I took my seat and chirped, "I'll tell the truth, nothing but the truth, and that's that. Can I have a cupcake now?"

"This is a courtroom, Miss Kellen, not a bakery."

"Court sessions would be so much better if they were also bakeries."

"She is most sincere about this," the angel said.

"I didn't need a verification of that but thank you. How old were you when you first went to a corrections facility, Miss Kellen?"

I shrugged. "As a visitor or a resident?"

"Resident, although I would like to know why you were a visitor," the judge replied.

"My mother took me to the parking lot of a detention center once. People like me belong in places like that. Since she couldn't drown me, I guess she wanted to make it clear what she thought of me. She wasn't wrong. I mean, look at me now."

"And your first time as a resident?"

"It's in the paperwork. I guess I was three or four. Maybe five. Or so I was told. It's sketchy, since I don't really remember much

of anything before my various residencies.
The first few weren't in prison. That was a
little later."

The judge's attention landed on the prosecuting attorney, "Esquire, I hope you have a
damned good explanation why she, as a child,
was in a correctional facility rather than an
orphanage. As the state's prosecuting resident, I trust you have reviewed everything
about her case? Including the increasing
probability of unfair child labor?"

The man had a decency to grimace. "It's
not my jurisdiction, Your Honor. I'm just
here for the cupcake case."

"False," the angel announced, and I shiv-
ered at the hostility in her tone. "Not a word
of that is true."

"Explain," the judge announced. "And
should another lie pass your lips, I will have
you ejected for contempt of court and you
will face perjury charges. You will not sabo-
tage this young lady's case with your lies.
Frankly, I'm disgusted you would even attempt to lie in the presence of an angel. I will
be filing to the association about this."

The prosecutor turned a rather intriguing
shade of gray-green. "I apologize, Your
Honor."

"I question your sincerity." Judge Davids
grunted, shook his head, and regarded the
angel with a scowl. "Your opinion?"

"He does not have the accused's interests at heart because he feels that people like her do not deserve to be rehabilitated. He feels that she is without value because she does not meet his personal ideals, and it is his mission to make certain she stays in correctional facilities where she belongs, as she at least serves a purpose there. If her parole terms are made in such a way that she has no hope of adhering to them, the state will continue to benefit from her incarceration."

The judge drummed his fingers on the polished wood surface in front of him. "I have crossed many fools in my time overseeing this courtroom, but you're one of the worst of the lot. You sit there, having heard the circumstances, yet still you believe that load of steaming drivel?"

"Most people call that shit, Your Honor," I said. "It's okay. He's probably one of those."

"Those?"

"Egotistical assholes who look down on people, especially women, whenever he crosses paths with them. He's probably one of those creeps who tries to blame a woman for being raped because he believes men aren't actually responsible for their own actions." I smiled my sweetest smile. "I've seen plenty of court sessions where petty, worthless scumbags stand there and blame the victims, so their guilty clients walk while the victim suffers. There ain't no justice in that, and I think it says a lot coming from me. I'm no shining example of morality, but even I understand that's wrong. You should have one of those unicorns stab him. He probably deserves it."

The stallion swung his head around to regard the prosecutor, flattened his ears, and snorted. A blob of slobber splattered onto the man's face.

"Okay. That's cool. Could you do that again?"

Apparently, unicorns could spit, and both had good aim, hitting the attorney in the face.

"That is the coolest thing I have ever seen happen during a trial. Like, the only way this could get better is if someone brought me a cupcake."

The angel disappeared in a flash of golden light.

"For some reason, I don't think she's gone off to get that jerk a towel. I mean, she might. She's an angel and all. What's the proper etiquette for thanking a pair of unicorns for doing me a big favor? I can't spit nearly as well as they can. Until now, I really didn't know unicorns could spit."

My attorney rubbed her brow, shook her head, and heaved a sigh.

The angel returned, and she held a cupcake in her hand, which she set on the stand in front of me. Pink powder sparkled on top of the white icing. "Using my own money, I purchased this for you. It is not a violation of your parole if someone who can legally acquire pixie dust, such as myself, gives it to you as a gift. It is low grade, and it won't do much more than ease some of your stress from being in court."

Cupcakes didn't exist in prison, and I'd never been out long enough to try one. I swallowed, staring at the confectionary offering with wide eyes. "I can really have this?"

"It was mine, and now it is yours to do with as you please."

I broke the cupcake into three parts, grabbed the two larger pieces, and scampered down from my seat and offered a share to each of the unicorns. I had no idea what to say to them, but without me having to say a word, they accepted my offering, eating out of my hand with their ears pricked forward. Only once they'd licked my palms clean did I return to my seat and wipe my hands off on my jeans before trying a bite.

Every now and then, we were rewarded for good behavior with sugar, usually in the form of a small packet meant to be added to a prized cup of coffee. The cupcake took everything I knew about sugar, turned it on its head, and punched me in the tongue. The pixie dust, even in such a small dose, helped.

"I just gave her something she has never

had before, something most in this room
would take for granted. Most would have
eaten the cupcake. After all, it is meant for
one person, correct? But instead of simply
eating it, she broke it into pieces and shared it
to two beings who had showed her an act of
kindness, however odd that act of kindness
may be; they came to her defense when she
was treated poorly. This is not a human beyond rehabilitation. This is not someone who
is malicious by default." The angel's attention
fell on the prosecutor. "You could learn a lot
from her. A dishonest human should not be
working to incarcerate an honest one. Perhaps she has made poor choices, but without
the base understanding of society you have,
how can you expect her to abide by society's
standards? No one has taught her. The system
has created her ignorance, and it is the responsibility of the system to cure her ignorance, although with men like you involved, it
comes as no surprise to me why I have been
summoned. Honesty is not one of your
virtues. You lack virtue in general. The court
would be wise to check deeper into your activities. Should you continue to obstruct, I am
sure I could assist this court with that."

"As far as threats go, that's a good one. I
mean, if an angel told me I was scum and
should go bugger off, I'd go bugger off, because angels are honest, and angels will do

exactly as threatened. They're not threats. They're promises."

"Most astute," the angel replied.

"I'm not the one on trial here!" the attorney blurted.

"Maybe you should be," my attorney replied.

The stallion kicked a hoof at the prosecutor's table, and while he didn't connect with the wood, the man recoiled, tipping over his chair and falling to the floor.

"Are you really sure I can't steal the stallion, Your Honor?"

"You don't need to steal him, Miss Kellen. I already told you you'll be responsible for his care following this session. The only question is how your parole will be handled in light of what we have learned. You have a lot to learn before you're ready to be integrated into society. You'll require someone to tutor you in common life skills."

"You mean like how money works?"

"Precisely."

"Is it really that important as long as I use it instead of just taking stuff?"

"It is."

"Well, that sounds like a problem."

"Here's what I'm going to do. I'm going to give you a six-month parole, during which you will be tutored. The terms of your parole will be simple. You are to keep the company of both unicorns without losing either one of them, and you will attend tutoring sessions as assigned."

"That sounds a little too simple," I replied, narrowing my eyes. "What's the catch?"

"Those unicorns are trouble. I wish you the best of luck. You're going to need it. In six months, we will evaluate your case, and I will request an angel for verification, as I'm of the opinion the state of North Carolina has been participating in child abuse and child labor, and they have used a government-hired attorney to hide the reality of this situation. Your punishment for the theft of a cupcake laced with pixie dust is to participate in a six-month rehabilitation program outside of prison, after which you will return for another hearing." Judge Davids lifted his gavel and cracked it against the block. "You're free to go, Miss Kellen. You will be required to check in with a parole officer of my choosing once a week. Do not forget to take your unicorns with you."

"But where will I go?" I asked, at a complete loss of what I was supposed to do.

Usually, the corrections officers dumped me at a temporary housing solution, which amounted to a room with a few bunks expected to be shared with other former inmates without anywhere else to live.

"The state has been making arrangements

for where the unicorns will reside. As their caretaker, you will have to stay with them."

"In wherever it is unicorns live?"

"Well, they won't be staying in a stall. They'll make excellent house guests, so don't worry about that. You'll be staying in a house in the country."

"A what?"

"A stall is where horses live, and I'll leave you to discover what the country is for yourself, as your record implies you've been limited to urban settings."

Life sounded complicated. "With all due respect, Your Honor, this sounds like a terrible idea. I have no idea what I'm doing."

"A tutor will be provided."

"What did that poor bastard do to deserve that?"

The judge sighed. "I'm sure your tutor will be a willing volunteer."

I doubted I would ever understand people or the court system. "But why?"

"I expect for the same reason you shared your cupcake with the unicorns, Miss Kellen." The judge rose, and the court clerk hurried through the formalities to bring the session to an end.

With a furrowed brow, I escaped the witness stand and returned to my attorney's table. "But what am I supposed to do now?"

"Well, we figure out what to do with your

two unicorns, and then I'll talk to the judge to find out where this residence is."

The angel laughed. "I believe the male unicorn expects to be ridden."

"No way. They can be ridden?" I regarded the large animals in surprise. "That doesn't seem safe. Or easy. How does one ride a unicorn?"

"The same way one rides a horse," the angel replied.

Engaging in a staring contest with a headless being took work, but I managed.

"You sit on his back, Layla," my attorney explained.

"But how?"

"You straddle him."

"That's not a helpful answer."

"I expect she'll have to experience it for herself," the angel said, her tone amused. "Life is about to become an adventure for you, Layla. I do recommend against stealing things in the future, though I expect you'll find things that don't technically belong to you finding their way into your hands. Just try to return them—for the most part."

"Did you just encourage me to steal stuff?"

"I am encouraging you to return the stuff you will inevitably steal as you try to adapt to your new living situation. It would be foolish of me to assume you will venture into the world without any incidents."

"For the most part?"

"Some things stolen you probably shouldn't return."

"Like what?"

"Hearts come to mind."

"If I steal a heart, the person will die, because you need your heart to live."

"Wrong type of heart," the angel replied.

As I didn't understand what she meant, I decided to somewhat change the subject. "Are you really sure I can't steal a unicorn?"

"You don't need to steal one, Layla. They're going with you of their own free will."

"I know good psychologists that work for the state. They might be able to help the unicorns return to sanity."

The angel sighed, and my lawyer laughed before saying, "They don't need a mental evaluation, Layla."

"Are you sure?"

"For the first time since this fiasco started, yes. I'm sure. They're unicorns. How much trouble can they be? It'll be a good experience learning how to take care of someone else, even if that someone has four hooves and can be ridden. I imagine it'll be pretty hard to screw up caring for a unicorn."

"The male one jumped pretty good when I slapped his ass."

The angel fluttered her wings, and she

giggled. "He was not expecting that, so you startled him most gloriously. Do continue to do things like that. It is good to teach him his place."

Then, in a flash of silvery light, the angel disappeared.

"Why do I need to teach him his place?"

"Good question. I suspect you'll find out soon enough. There's a sitting area outside, so let's go there and see about what needs to happen to have you moved to your new home. Is there anything you need retrieved for you?"

I stared at her. "What do you mean?"

"Personal possessions."

"Like my toothbrush?"

"Oh, dear. This is going to be even more of a challenge than I thought. Come along, Layla. There's no time better than the present."

The unicorns followed us, and whenever I snuck peeks at the pair, the male glared at me with his ears turned back. "I pissed off the male."

"I'm sure he'll be fine. Everything I've read about unicorns implies they're very intelligent. I don't know if they can speak English, but I expect you'll find out soon enough."

"Why does that sound threatening?"

"It sounds threatening because you're smart and being followed by two unicorns, which are horses with weapons attached to their heads."

I regarded the male with narrowed eyes. "If you even think about stabbing me with that weapon attached to your head, I will cut it off. We clear?"

He lifted his head and snorted at me. I considered myself fortunate he didn't spit in my face.

"And don't you spit on me, either. It's probable you're going to starve to death unless I can steal what you need, because right now, the details of what the hell I'm supposed to do with you are hazy at best."

"Don't worry, Layla. We'll sort everything out, and you won't have to steal anything to feed them."

"Are you sure?"

"I sure hope so, because I'm still stuck on where the state found two unicorns in the first place."

"Personally, I think only an idiot would assign me as their caretaker."

"I just hope I can teach you enough about life in society before you leave the courthouse today to get you started, without it being a disaster from the first day."

"I wish you luck. I'm pretty sure you're going to need it."

THREE

A STATE WORKER WITH A BRIEFCASE, which
he handed to me, came an hour after the trial's conclusion. "That has everything you'll
need to settle."

Considering my reading skills were only a
little better than my math skills, I held the
briefcase out to my attorney.

"Please tell me you've been reading the
documents you've been signing, Layla."

"If I told you that, I'd be lying. I do know
how to spell my name, and in my defense, I
mostly have the basics covered. Those documents just use excessively stupid words."

"We tend to call that legal jargon."

"I think I'll stick with excessively stupid
words."

As though sensing my attorney might turn
on him and kill him with the power of her
voice alone, the state worker fled. His flight

annoyed both unicorns into stomping their hooves and snorting.

My attorney cracked open the briefcase and spread out papers across the table. I spotted one of the cards they liked to give me whenever I escaped prison for a few days. Pointing at it, I asked, "So, that thing becomes money?"

"It's a debit card. It takes the money you want to pay with from an account that contains the money you've earned. You can only spend the amount of money you've earned from that account."

"Let me guess. I'm going to need math and numbers to understand how that all works."

"Essentially."

"Great. And counting to ten ten times isn't going to cut it, is it?"

"Not even remotely."

"All right. We may as well get this over with. What else are you going to tell me that I'm not going to like?"

"I'm pretty sure the entire briefcase is going to be like that, but everything will be things you should know. We'll start with the rental agreement."

"The what?"

"Rental agreements are how people loan a property to someone else. You pay rent to live in a place you don't own. According to this paper, the state will be paying your rent for a period of six months, after which you'll have to move somewhere else or take on the burden of payments."

"Why are they paying this rent for me?"

"I'm assuming the judge decided the state would be doing that because they used you as child labor illegally, and angelic verification gives him a lot of rights to make such edicts. In this case, he found the state guilty and you innocent, so the state will have to pay you for their crimes. It seems the state wasted no time agreeing to some of the judge's terms; the signature on this is from today, so I'm assuming the judge contacted another angel and fast-tracked processing. Usually, this sort of thing takes months. They've gone and done my job for me, honestly."

"They have?"

"In this case, I'd be recommending you press charges, and another attorney, a prosecutor from another state, would come in and handle the trial. I would still be available for you, but as you're no longer the defendant, the nature of the case changes substantially."

"The more you tell me, the less I like it. Is that normal?"

"Well, I am a lawyer. That is often part of my job, telling people things they don't want to hear. In your case, once you are able to figure out how everything works, you'll be much better off. The gaps in your education are a major concern."

I pointed at the unicorns. "I bet they could teach me."

"I'm not sure they're formally educated on the ways of the human world."

"They are probably more educated about it than I am."

"Pardon my intrusion," a deep-voiced man said before strolling into the room. My brows shot up. While an angel made sense visiting a court, the last thing I expected was a hotter than sin, dark-skinned beauty of a man strolling in sporting a tail and leathery wings. "I'm here to provide instruction for a Layla Kellen?"

The stallion's ears pinned back, and he lashed his tail while his sister whinnied, a sound reminding me of laughter.

I had no idea what she found funny, although she might have reason to laugh at me if I couldn't restrain myself from drooling.

Swallowing several times, I turned to my lawyer, pointed at the man, and blurted, "I don't know what he is or what I'm supposed to do with him, but can I steal him?"

She laughed. "I don't think any theft is required. He's an incubus, Layla. He'd probably go with you willingly if you wanted. If you don't want him, I certainly wouldn't mind taking him home to my husband."

Holy hell. After a brief but serious moment of consideration, I decided I wasn't interested in sharing a man, even a man of a different, albeit sexy, species. "I thought I needed help with math, not sexual deviance." Even I had heard of incubi and what they could do to men and women. The stories in prison were enough to scorch my virgin ears.

"I'm paying back an owed favor, and I assure you, I'm not here to educate you on any acts of sexual deviance."

"I can't tell if I'm disappointed or relieved."

"Go with relieved. I'm not your type."

I tilted my head. "You're not?"

"You're the kind to dedicate and expect dedication in return. You'd spend half your time beating me for straying, and the other half trying to convince me to stick around, and you'd be a mess by the end of the first week. While I usually enjoy virgins, I'd rather avoid nightly beatings for straying."

"I don't think I'd actually beat you." I furrowed my brow, considering the situation. "Would I?"

"You would because I'd like it."

Damn. My eyes widened. "What would I be beating you with?"

"Probably a paddle. They make it hurt better."

My attorney snickered. "He's toying with

you, Layla. It's what they do. He'll cause you problems the entire time he's tutoring you."

The stallion snorted and stamped his hoof.

The incubus raised a brow. "Didn't I just say I wasn't interested? If you want to compete, you're just going to have to stop prancing around as a horse with a penis plastered onto your forehead."

While I'd dodged useful education in prison, I'd had my fair share of exposure to rowdy men and their penises. That story had always ended the same way, with them enduring pain and suffering while I'd returned to my cell, swearing I'd cut off the next one someone brought near me without invitation.

I'd gotten a reputation as a ball buster, and men had decided they would rather remain intact, opting to leave me alone.

"His horn looks nothing like a penis," I announced.

My attorney cracked up laughing. "It really doesn't. I take it incubi don't get along well with unicorns."

"They're almost as prissy as angels when they aren't trying to take over the world."

"Unicorns are trying to take over the world?" I asked, regarding the brother and sister with interest. "How does a unicorn try to take over the world?"

"I think she's planning on just stealing

things and building an empire based on wealth and taking over that way. He's on a slightly different mission." The incubus shrugged. "You're going to have your hands full."

"Does she want help? Because that sounds like something I'd be good at."

"No," my attorney said, slapping a stack of papers against the table to get my attention. "You're reforming. That means you can't help the unicorn steal things."

"Why not?"

"Theft is wrong, Layla."

"So is math," I muttered. "But people are expecting me to learn how numbers work anyway."

"Call me Westin. In addition to teaching you the basics of mathematics, I've been asked to take you to your new residence and show you how you'll be expected to care for yourself and your companions."

"What did they do to deserve this? I mean, they probably had to do some hefty crime to get stuck with me as their caretaker."

"Not precisely, but it amuses me thinking of unicorns as criminals. They're disgustingly good-natured creatures most of the time. Then again, that one does want to take over the world, and the other has even more nefarious plans. Actually, I'm rather impressed. They're like pure little bundles of evil."

Oh. Right. Westin counted as a demon or a devil or something like that. "That makes no sense. How can anyone be pure and evil? Are you going to try to kill the unicorns? Or are they going to try to kill you? Because honestly, while fights can be entertaining, I get pretty pissy if I have to break them up. I'm also not sure how I'd break up a fight between a pair of unicorns and an incubus."

"Very carefully. Honestly, you could accomplish such a thing taking off your shirt," Westin replied. "Breasts are so much better than fights, if I do say so myself."

The stallion flicked an ear forward, which I interpreted as a general interest in breasts, too. I regarded mine with a frown. "They mostly just get in the way and cost the state a fortune. Or, that's what the prison supervisors say while complaining when they're forced to provide new bras."

My attorney sighed. "Clothing shopping is going to be a requirement, Mr. Westin."

"Just Westin, please. I recommend you request a complete auditing of Miss Kellen's file while I handle her living arrangements and settling her and her companions. Despite my species, you'll find I'm quite capable and nurturing when the situation requires it. I volunteered as I do enjoy humanitarian services and not just the kind that ends with everyone being a little happier for a while. My contact recommended me, as I might be a grounding influence."

"Am I the only one who finds this whole idea to be disturbing? Unless I'm being trained on how to take over the world with a unicorn. That sounds interesting, especially as you mentioned it involved a lot of money. If I have a lot of money, I can just use the card and not have to worry about the math, right?"

The attorney and the incubus exchanged long looks.

"What? It seemed perfectly sensible to me."

"She really has no idea about the value of money, does she?"

"Not a clue. Try not to overwhelm her too much. She had her first cupcake today, and when she found out she could work an hour to earn one topped with pixie dust, her expression concerned me. She might become a workaholic if she's paid in cupcakes."

Westin considered me, making a thoughtful noise in his throat. "I was asked to help her find a career that suits her. I was not told she couldn't become a criminal mastermind."

"The idea is to integrate her into society, not send her back to prison."

"She'd only go to prison if she got caught."

"Can we try something legal for once?

And honestly, that I just asked that question shocks even me."

"And on that happy note, I'll leave you to Westin. I want to make sure I can get everything I need to help you press charges against the state and get the wheels in motion for that. I'd rather do it while the judge is likely to be cooperative so I can get his input on how to proceed. Are you all right with that, Layla?"

"As long as he reads those papers for me."

"She can't read?" Westin asked.

"It's going to be an interesting set of charges the state will face for her incarceration. This morning, I expected a run of the mill case. Well, that's not what I got. But it'll be a challenge, and I'm all right with that. I'm only sad I opted to be a defense attorney rather than a prosecutor. I'd love to spank the defense on this one." My attorney handed Westin a card. "Call me if there are any issues. I'd also like if you would get Layla set up with a phone and plug my number into her contacts so she can contact me herself if needed."

"I feel I have been tricked, but I have been tricked in such a way I must respect the efforts gone into putting me in this situation. Very well. Layla, you do not have a driver's license?"

"Do you think they'd actually allow the inmates to drive the bus?" I countered.

"The answer to that is no. It's a privilege the incarcerated do not enjoy. She won't pass a test, anyway. She couldn't read the questions to answer them, if my guess is correct."

"I would resent your comment, except it's true. I guess I have to learn how to read the damned excessively stupid words, don't I?"

"Yes," my attorney replied.

"Well, shit."

"With that out of the way, I have a lot of work to do if I want to leave the courthouse today. I wish you the best of luck, Layla. Please call me if there's any issues, and I will check in with you as soon as I have something concrete."

My attorney packed up her suitcase, leaving a disconcerting number of papers on the table. I regarded them with disdain.

"You have no idea what your attorney's name is, do you?"

"Should I?"

"Usually, humans do like to know the name of the people defending them in court."

Huh. "But why? It's not like they stick around or really care what happens to me. I mean, that's just how it is. Most attorneys see my record and laugh. I think she was too stunned and horrified to laugh, and I figured why bring names into it? I'm sure her name was written on one of the papers I signed without reading."

"Her name is Kelly."

"Well, why didn't she just say so rather than expecting me to read it off a stupid piece of paper?"

The incubus stared at the unicorns. "You both willingly volunteered for this? You are better beings than I."

Laughing, I grabbed the nearest stack of papers. "Now that I have horrified even a demon-devil thing, let's begin with these papers. What do they say, and why are they important?"

"Heaven help me," the incubus muttered before sitting down and taking the sheets out of my hand. "This is the court order authorizing your immediate release from prison and authorizing a state representative, in this case, me, to assist you with whatever you need to make it possible for you to meet your parole terms. Your parole terms are also defined in this document as successfully caring for these two unicorns."

"Do they have names, or will I be calling them Pissy and Prissy?"

"Can we just call them Pissy and Prissy anyway?"

"Not if their names are written down on one of these papers, and if I learn to read and find out you lied to me about their names, I will insert Pissy's horn up your ass."

"Which one is Pissy?"

"The male, since he's been pissy the entire court session. The other one is Prissy because she looked offended that she had to deal with mere humans."

"To be fair, dealing with mere humans can be quite the drag, so try not to judge her too harshly," Westin replied. "His name is Dean, and his sister's name is Xena."

"Okay. Xena I can understand as a name for a unicorn. That's exotic and rather pretty. But Dean? You may as well prance him out and showcase him as the most normal damned thing in North Carolina. Bean is more interesting than Dean, so I'm calling him Bean."

"That's not how names work, Layla."

"It is now."

"Okay then. Moving on." Westin tossed the sheets aside and picked up a new stack. "This one is a list of expenses the state will cover while it investigates your earnings issue. It is being paid out as compensation for mistreatment, which has been verified by an angel. I'm not going to waste my time reading the numbers to you right now, as they won't mean anything without an understanding of how math works."

"That is the most sensible thing anyone has said to me today."

"Just because I'm delaying the explanation of the specifics does not mean you're getting out of learning what everything means."

"Okay. That's fair. I think. What else are all these papers for?"

The tallest stack proved to be a condensed listing of all charges, and the judge had highlighted all questionable punishments. "What does it mean by questionable?"

"You were sentenced to a year for pilfering a sandwich. The maximum penalty for North Carolina for the pilfering of something valued below a thousand dollars is a hundred and fifty days, and it should have been issued as community service rather than imprisonment." Westin sorted through the papers, spreading them out. He pulled out a phone from his pocket and tapped at the screen. "According to this, you were unlawfully detailed for a period of at least five and a half years of excess sentencing."

"Should I assume that is a lot? I really don't pay a lot of attention to how much time passes. There's no point, you know?"

"Yes, it is a long time."

"Okay. What does this mean for me?"

"It means the state will owe you a lot in damages, compensation, and so on. It also means that there will be a lot of people answering some uncomfortable questions in the near future, as the majority of your cases were handled by a limited number of judges and attorneys. A note here says Judge Davids was brought in to review your case on special request."

"Who made the request?"

"That I can't tell you. It's just a notation. But the notation explains why he was able to get so many concessions from the state in such a short period of time. It's pretty obvious to any sane individual your cases have been grossly mishandled."

"Am I the only one who is confused about all this? Why me?"

"I'm most certainly confused. I'm not sure what skills you have that someone in the prison system could possibly want."

"I can sew."

"Unless you're turning thread to gold, that's not really a skill worth gaming the system over."

"Why not?"

"Sewing can be automated with machines for much cheaper than having someone hand sew something. Machines can even embroider."

"Oh! I've done that. I like the days I can embroider. I think it's fun. I like the colors and making pretty artwork. The last time I embroidered, I got to recreate a painting. It took me a while, but I did a fantastic job. I've done some paintings, too."

Westin set the papers down, and his expression turned curious. "What sort of painting did you do?"

"The kind you use a brush for. I'd be given a picture and told to paint it. So I did."

"Exactly?"

"Well, yes. That is the point."

"Art counterfeiting is a big business. A big and very illegal business, Layla."

"Huh. Does that mean I'm good at it?"

"That's a very good question. If you're good at painting, you could make a career out of that, especially if you're good enough to counterfeit a painting."

"But what would I paint?"

"Anything you wanted. You could go outside and paint what you see, and if the painting is good enough, someone will buy it. People will buy art simply for the reason they like it."

"Oh. Is art valuable?"

"If you were painting counterfeit art being passed off as the real thing, let's just say that one painting would make a crook very, very rich. That's more likely the reason than your sewing, unless you're sewing something that's also a counterfeit of some sort. Give me a minute." Westin tapped the screen of his phone before holding it to his ear. "Your Honor, I think I've figured out why they wanted to keep Miss Kellen incarcerated. When we were discussing life skills, she told

me she would sew, and when I said it was unlikely that would be worth gaming the system
over, she told me she's recreated various
paintings, both in embroidery and as new
paintings. When I asked her if she was recre-
ating exact duplicates, she said, rather directly, that was the point. You may want to
get angelic verification of what's going on, as
there might be an art counterfeiting ring
lurking in the prison system, and Miss Kellen
might be one of their skilled laborers they'd
rather not have leave the system."

The unicorns listened with interest, and
the stallion looked ready to spit at someone.
"Please don't spit on the incubus, Dean the
Bean. Or on me, for that matter. I don't have
any other duds."

"We'll take care of your clothing situation
once we're done here," Westin informed me.

"How? Do we have to steal new duds?"

"No. You'll buy them."

"Shit. I'm going to have to count?"

"No. I'll count and show you how to use
your card properly, and I'll explain how the
counting works after the fact. If I try to explain it beforehand, we'll never leave the
store."

"This sounds unfairly complicated."

"Sorry, Your Honor. Miss Kellen is under-
standably confused about how we'll be pro-
ceeding. If this is a counterfeiting ring, she

will require protection—more protection than a pair of unicorns and myself can provide. My initial impression is that, due to the number of judges and attorneys potentially involved, this is a well-established ring involving a great deal of money. I'll ask her." Westin sighed. "Layla, how long have you been painting?"

"I guess when I first got there. They needed something for me to do, because I was too little to use the machines like the older kids in the system. I liked the painting." I frowned. "I did something wrong, didn't I?"

"No. You didn't do anything wrong. It's just going to make this complicated mess even more complicated, and this job wasn't as simple as I thought it would be. Oh, well. At least I won't get bored."

"Heaven forbid," I muttered.

Dean kicked a hoof and spit on the far wall. All things considered, I agreed with his general opinion, and as I hadn't asked him to refrain from spitting entirely, I held my peace.

I wanted to do something a lot worse than spit.

"Hey, Westin?"

"Yes, Layla?"

"Is stabbing these assholes illegal?"

"Unfortunately, it is."

"Well, that's a bummer. If I can't stab

them, can I burn them?"

"No, you can't burn them."

"Run them over in a stolen prison bus?"

"Even if you used your own bus, it would still be illegal. Stealing the prison bus would just make it even more illegal."

"I guess drowning them is out, too."

"You're catching on."

"What can I do?"

"Very little, I'm afraid. That's the problem with humans. Justice isn't usually all that just. I'd go with the fire route, personally, and make it a very slow roast. Alas, that's illegal. Foolishness, if you ask me."

Both unicorns sighed.

"I don't think the unicorns like the idea of a slow roast, Westin."

"Neither does the judge on the phone with me. I can't imagine why."

"Me, neither. So, what's next?"

"Let me finish this call, and we'll figure the rest out. We won't be stealing anything, however. I recommend keeping your hands in your pockets to mitigate any temptation. Let's get you through your first day of freedom without adding another petty misdemeanor to your list."

While I thought the incubus was a fool to ask for a miracle, I'd give putting my hands in my pockets a try. Maybe it would help.

I had my doubts, but I would try.

FOUR

You can't shank someone with your clothing.

WESTIN, Judge Davids, an angel, and a herd of attorneys had a field day with the story of how I'd sewn, embroidered, and painted my way to a major felony, one I wouldn't face charges for, as I'd had no way of knowing duplicating paintings counted as a serious crime. I found the fiasco amusing while the unicorns napped.

After several hours of answering questions and one stint of having an angel rummage through my memories to confirm I could do as I claimed, the judge ordered Westin to take me to my new residence.

The angel's sifting through my memories left me with a headache, and by the time we got around to shopping for new clothes, I was too damned tired to steal anything. I kept my hands to myself, handed the magical money-providing card to the store clerk, and fol-

lowed Westin's instructions on how to fi-
nalize the payment.

"In bad news, the delays at the courthouse
have ruined my plans. In worse news, most
hotels aren't going to be keen on welcoming
unicorns in their rooms, so you two free-
loaders are going to have to shift and make
yourselves useful—or attach rockets to your
ass and run us halfway across the state. While
I know how to ride, Layla does not."

"They can shift?" I regarded the unicorns
with interest. "I thought unicorns were just,
well, fancy horses with horns. I guess that
means they really do speak English?"

"They speak English. It wouldn't surprise
me if they're fluent in several languages. Unicorns are quick learners, although they do
tend to be prudes. They also tend to mate for
life, and that puts a crimp in my style. I certainly wouldn't pick a unicorn. I'd be expected to stick around."

"How tragic."

"It really is."

Dean snorted, and I recognized the gruff
sound in his throat as him preparing to spit. I
grabbed my heaviest bag and prepared to
wage war. "Go ahead and try me. I'll shank
you with my clothes."

"You can't shank someone with your
clothing, Layla."

"Watch me."

After careful consideration, the stallion turned his head and refrained from snorting —or spitting.

"That's right, buddy. Keep on walking. I meant it. Try me. I really will put your furry ass in your place."

"We're going to have to work on your aggression," Westin announced.

"Why? It's been useful. Nobody screwed around with me in prison. The first time I shanked someone with a metal bowl, they learned they better be ready for a fight. And trust me, it takes a lot of effort to shank somebody with a metal bowl."

"I see we're going to have to have a talk about sanctioned uses of violence."

"I don't shank anyone who doesn't start something with me first. The unicorn was going to spit on me. If he spits on me, his furry ass is getting a smackdown."

"You should just tell him he's not a llama."

"I don't think he'll care. Bean does not seem to be a very caring unicorn unless he's going after idiot attorneys. But I already paid my dues there. I shared my cupcake with them."

Westin shook his head. "Please just shift. It's not like you were going to hide your secret forever. She would've figured it out when she couldn't figure out where the hell you two were going to the bathroom without leaving piles of shit everywhere for her to clean up."

I thought about that. "That's a good point. A unicorn can't use a toilet."

"Well, I'm sure they could, but they'd have to be really careful with their aim, and it would end in a clogged toilet."

"I really will shank them with my clothes if they clog the toilet. I've unclogged toilets before, and that is not one of my favorite jobs."

"Then we're agreed. The unicorns will shift, you'll be properly introduced, and we'll get this show on the road tomorrow because we're not getting anywhere tonight. For some reason, there's a lack of licensed drivers among us."

"You don't have a license?"

"Why drive when I can teleport?"

"That's cheating."

"I'm an incubus. That's what I do."

AS UNICORNS WERE white and gray, I expected pasty humans to go with their pale coats. Xena showed up first, and my brows shot up at the dark tone of her skin, the closest to black I'd ever seen in a living, breathing person without the help of paint. She'd even found a tight shirt and jeans the perfect match of her skin. She looked me over with her blue eyes, and I got the feeling she found me lacking in every way.

"You need a lot of work. How am I going to take over the world if I have to hold your hand all the damned time?" she asked, and she put her hands on her hips.

"Remember what I said about shanking you with my clothes?"

"I do."

"I have multiple techniques I can use to shank you with this bag of clothes. There will be no attempts to take over the world while I'm on parole. If I go to prison again, I want it to be for something better than shanking a stubborn ass unicorn with my jeans."

"Is there any reason you decided to be an ebony beauty today, Xena?"

"You're hot, and I've been itching to tame an incubus."

Westin disappeared.

"Okay. Well, it's not like he was going to teach me how math works or English or anything. Way to go, Xena."

"You don't need math skills when you do what I say while we take over the world. That said, he ran faster than I expected. It's not like I would've tamed him for mating purposes. Incubi might be good at sex, but they're a lot of work outside of bed, and what woman has time for that nonsense?"

I had no idea. "And where's your brother?"

"Trying to make himself even half as pretty as me so he can impress you, probably. That's what stallions do around interesting mares. Er, women." Xena shrugged. "All stallions are obnoxious until they've settled down. You may just want to beat him off with a stick. Otherwise, he'll stick around, and as his sister, I can promise you it's annoying."

"By my parole terms, you both have to stick around for a period of six months."

"Well, you're getting the short end of that deal."

"Well, it is parole. That's how it works. It's a short end of the deal, but at least it's the short end of the deal dealt with outside of prison. Granted, the longest I've successfully stayed out of jail has been a day. Less than that, but counting the hours was too much work."

"You're rather cheerful about all of this."

"What else should I do? Pity myself? I mean, how many people can claim they shanked an overly amorous asshole with a metal bowl?"

"Not many," she conceded.

"There you go. I might not be your usual bitch, but I'm an interesting one."

"Would you like some help shanking my brother? I feel like he should be punished for getting us into this. I was promised excitement and adventure, not this."

"What do you mean by this?"

"Prancing around North Carolina with a kleptomaniac drug addict with a temper issue and a generalized malfunction."

I considered her stance, and realistically, I couldn't argue with her except on one point. "I cleaned up, so can we scratch the drug addict part from the record?"

"Sure. Okay. That's fair. You have a temper issue with a generalized malfunction."

"And a kleptomaniac's restraint."

"You like that phrase too much."

"What can I say? It's the simple things in life."

Xena shook her head. "Nope. Not anymore. If we're going to take over the world, those simple ways have to go. We're not going to take over the world being simple. We're going to be elaborate and glorious."

At long last, I'd found someone crazier than I was. "Pitch me again in six months and a day, all right?"

"I am willing to compromise on this. Six months and a day, then. That might be enough time to teach you everything that's important."

"Let me guess. You only view things that help you take over the world as important."

"You would be correct. But money, how

money works, and how to make more money are important skills, so I will teach you."

"And what is Dean's malfunction again?"

"He is single and male."

"I'm single but not male. And? You're single and not male."

"The not male part of things is important. We're sensible creatures. Males are not."

"That seems a little harsh."

"You'll learn soon enough, Layla. Men want women for one of five things."

I worried for my sanity, but my curiosity reared its ugly head. "What five things?"

"Sex, sex, sex, sex, and food."

"I may not be math inclined, but I have five fingers on my hand, and that's two things, with one of those things repeated."

"Well, you're not completely hopeless. Good. In actuality, it's sex, food, babies, someone to protect, and someone to pamper. Stallions are all about the protecting and the pampering, but they really enjoy sex, food, and babies, too. Really, there's worse things in life than an attentive stallion."

I seriously doubted her opinion held much ground in the real world, but I wouldn't poke the crazy with a stick and point that out to her. Fortunately, she'd left me with a safe opening. "There are things worse than an attentive stallion? Like what?"

"Cowardly incubi. Just because we settle

down for life when we do doesn't mean we don't test the waters first, and trust me on this one, Layla. You want a man who rocks your world in bed *and* out of it. Of course, it's a challenge to get a unicorn in bed in the first place, and if you've jumped through all those hoops, chances are, the unicorn is going to keep you, but we do not immediately bond with the first person we screw. I most certainly am not a virgin. I just haven't found a stallion who rocks my world in and out of bed. That incubus? He'd rock my world in bed, but I suspect he'd be rather useless outside of it."

I feared my sanity would not survive the parole process, but as I saw no other choice in the matter, I smiled and nodded. After six months, I'd take everything the woman had to offer, run for the hills, and try to stay on the right side of the law for a change.

I just had to survive through six months trying to herd a pair of unicorns.

I sure hoped Heaven would help me, because I needed all the help I could get.

IN RETROSPECT, I shouldn't have assumed that because Xena was a black woman that Dean would also be black. People came in all shapes, sizes, and colors, and Dean's skin was a sun-kissed bronze tone. Like his sister, he had black hair, but instead of tight curls, he had more of a fluffy, short-cropped mane that tempted me to run my fingers through it.

I didn't. I deserved a cupcake for controlling one of my impulses for a change.

Unlike his sister, Dean wore a suit, which hugged his frame and promised he had a lean and fit body.

All in all, I'd eat a cupcake off his chest without regret.

Damn. A cupcake sounded good.

To take my mind off my first cupcake, I frowned and considered the siblings. "All right. Please explain why he's some Mediterranean god and you're an African goddess, please. I'm confused. I thought people came out looking like their parents."

"You're actually right; humans usually do resemble their parents. Unicorns aren't like that. I was born in Africa, and he was born in Greece. We take on the traits of our birth places. He really is my brother. Full brother, too. Mom and Dad are probably trying to repopulate Ireland at this point; turns out they like being pampered, and there are a lot of people who really like unicorns in the British Isles, but they much prefer Ireland. They call us at least once a week asking when we'll settle down. I told our mother I'd consider it after I finished taking over the world." Xena laughed. "It's a work in progress, but I'm feeling much better about my odds now. The next few months will be interesting."

Okay. Unicorns confused me, but if I had to deal with odd parole terms, at least I'd be surrounded by beautiful, albeit strange, people. "Is all that stuff about women taking longer to get ready for anything not true, then?"

"I was born perfect. I don't need to do anything to be perfect. Dean? Dean has a long way to go. I mean, look at him. He looks like a stone carver got drunk and tried to chisel a pimp but made him instead."

I'd met more than a few pimps in prison, and they tended to make the most fuss if they gave me a reason to shank them. I'd only had to beat two pimps before they'd figured out to leave me alone. If the one chair hadn't come loose from the floor, the second pimp might've gotten off a lot lighter, but I'd enjoyed trying to insert a chair leg up his ass.

Hmm. Maybe there was something to me needing to take slightly less violent approaches to solving my life's problems.

On second thought, no. I'd definitely shove another chair up a pimp's ass.

While Xena considered her brother an artist's failure, I couldn't spot any defects or deformities. He had a softer jawline than I expected from most men, but he could give the incubus a run for his money and possibly win in a competition. "He doesn't seem to be missing any parts, and they're all in the right places."

"Compared to me, he is but a worm in the soil of life."

"Thanks, Xena. I'm so glad you care."

Unlike Westin, whose voice had a tendency to rumble, Dean's voice came in at the middle of the road, a rather pleasant change from most men I'd encountered in prison. For whatever reason, the men in prison tried to sound deep and intimidating right up until I gave them lessons in being a soprano.

"It helps you build character. Unlike me, you need all the help you can get."

"I can't tell if she likes or hates you. In prison, that kind of talk is the prelude to a fight, one I'd usually have to break up if the guards were slacking off. I really don't like breaking up fights. Bloody knuckles hurt."

"That's her way of telling me she loves me and wishes she wasn't my sister. Good stallions are hard to find, and she was born with the misfortune of not being eligible to compete for my attention. Us stallions have an edge on human males. We're very attentive."

"I hate that we're an endangered species." Xena stomped her foot. "Do you know how much damned work it is to convert a human male into a stallion? No! No, you don't. That's because you're out for a human, and you don't care if she's converted."

Dean sighed and shook his head. "Your mouth runneth over, Xena."

"Damn. It really is, isn't it?"

I had questions, but I was somewhat terrified of the answers the crazy pair might give me. What the hell did she mean by convert? I decided I'd ignore their casual discussion of their future love lives, as I'd gone out of my way to avoid sex with creeps, which the prison system had in vast quantities. "I have this card, I'm still not really clear on how to use it, and I have clothes. Where do I use this card to get something to eat without stealing it, and where do I use this card to sleep tonight? I mean, I've done the alley thing once. It was not comfortable, but it was free. Can we skip that? I'm assuming there are ways to use the card to sleep somewhere comfortable. But that's just an assumption."

"Yes, we can get a room at a hotel, and yes, we can go somewhere for dinner," Dean replied. "Also, if you ignore my sister, it drives her crazy. If we're really lucky, we'll get to watch her implode. Patience is not one of her virtues."

I doubted Xena had many virtues at all. Actually, I thought she'd fit in pretty well with the inmates at most prisons I'd been to.

"I guess all those stories about unicorns only liking virgins is also bullshit?"

"I know a unicorn who likes virgins for lunch," Xena announced.

I'd heard that innuendo plenty of times, and I narrowed my eyes. "Figuratively or literally?"

"Not with ketchup. He's more of the whipped cream and handcuffs type. He got roped by one of those virgins, and he deserved it."

"Roped?"

"They now have six foals, and he's since converted her. That was a fight that took him quite the while, as she rather liked being a human who'd whipped a stud into shape and made him dance to her tune. But attentive stallions are persistent stallions, and he eventually got his way. They had a good track record, though. All of their foals turned out unicorns despite her being human. Impressive really. We're an endangered species because it's hard for the mares to foal, and well, the human mares don't necessarily toss unicorns. Mom is determined, though."

"I'm afraid to ask."

"We have four brothers and fourteen sisters," Dean replied. "Mom and Dad like to spread the love, so they try to have a foal or two in every country. Personally, I think they've lost their minds, since there's not a whole lot of our kind around, so we're stuck trying to convert our partners."

"Please explain what you mean by convert."

Xena shrugged. "With enough work, we can change someone from human, or another species, into a unicorn. I guess we evolved since we have shitty luck reproducing. Well, part of that is our own damned fault. We live a long time, so why breed like bunnies? Humans don't live as long, so they tend to have a bunch of children all at one time. We don't do that. We take our sweet time about reproducing usually, and then we tip-toe around it, and then we're old and no longer interested in having foals. Mom's foal obsessed, and she's absolutely unhappy unless she has a foal around, so she's constantly seducing our father. He likes it, because well, he's an attentive stallion."

"And there goes all of my preconceived notions about the purity of unicorns."

"It's okay. Your preconceived notions were boring anyway. The reality is far worse. We're, frankly, rather dull. I mean, look at me. I'm going to take over the world because I'm bored."

I pointed at Dean. "And what's his excuse?"

"He's a male, Layla. We just went over this."

"Xena, what nonsense have you been telling her?"

"That attentive stallions want women for food, sex, babies, to protect, and to pamper."

Heaving a sigh, Dean bowed his head. "While some of that is true, you're missing a few important things."

"I am?"

"We aren't eating our women. We eat regular food."

Xena leered at her brother.

"You're a disgusting pervert."

"I am. But I meant a stallion's duties include feeding her. To *provide* food."

"Well, why didn't you say that, you little idiot?"

"I just did, moron!"

"Can my card buy you both some common sense?" I asked, digging out the plastic rectangle that held the key to my future. "Does this card have enough money to buy such a thing?"

"Probably not," Xena admitted. "But where's the fun in being common?"

"All right. Focus. Dinner and hotel. In that order. I think I've reached my threshold of unicorn insanity for one day. Both of you, please behave. You already drove off the incubus who was supposed to be teaching me important things."

"He's an incubus, Layla. He'd teach you

math by having you count the number of times he made you scream his name. That's what incubi do." Xena rolled her eyes and pointed down the street. "I saw a restaurant that way. We can start teaching you how math works while we eat dinner. We need to start somewhere and counting grains of rice is a good place to start."

While I figured I'd done *something* during my incarceration to deserve dealing with a pair of rowdy unicorns, I already wanted to beg for forgiveness or a quick trip back to prison.

I understood prison.

I didn't understand unicorns.

FIVE

Asshole unicorns.

I UNDERSTOOD MORE about math than I'd thought. It was like someone had, over the course of my life, established the basic framework for mathematics without bothering to teach me how everything connected together. Xena provided those connections, and when it clicked, things started fitting into place.

I almost liked math until she gave me the menu and wanted me to make sense of the numbers. The menu proved a challenge, as the existence of the decimal point vexed me.

While I struggled to make sense of the menu and its evil numbers, Xena ordered half of the restaurant, Dean ordered the other half, and both took turns ordering for me. Then, since he hadn't been evil enough ordering half the restaurant, Dean made the waiter let us keep one of the menus so they could continue torturing me with it.

Asshole unicorns.

"Everything has a value," Xena announced, holding up one of the newly arrived egg rolls. "This egg roll is valued at two dollars. Two dollars is two hundred pennies. How many pennies are in a single dollar?"

As I had five fingers, and I understood the relationship between one and two, I discovered I could determine how many pennies were in a dollar with little effort. "One hundred pennies."

"Correct. For correctly answering the question, you may eat this egg roll." Xena placed it on my plate, and she dribbled some of the orange sauce beside the roll. "Dip it in that and see if you like it. I have just made a rule. Every time you correctly answer a math question, you get to eat. Otherwise, you starve."

"You are not going to starve Layla while teaching her math." Dean snagged another egg roll and placed it on my plate. "If you're hungry, eat. There will be no food restrictions associated with math skills, so can it, Xena."

"Why are you ruining all my fun?"

"Because your fun encroaches on Layla discovering Chinese food."

"Oh. Right. You've never had this before, have you?"

I regarded the egg roll warily. "I don't even know how I'm supposed to eat this."

"Dip the end, either one, into the sauce. Insert the end into your mouth, bite off enough you can chew." Xena grabbed one and demonstrated. I followed her lead, and I discovered that whatever the hell was in one, it tasted even better than the cupcake. "Now, dip it again, and repeat until you have put the entire egg roll into your stomach where it belongs."

"I'll make sure we get actual utensils, as I expect the chopsticks would pose a problem."

I expected a lot would pose problems for me in the near future. "Is this how people usually eat?"

While I'd thought my question to be a sane one, both unicorns stared at me with dismay before staring at each other.

Dean recovered first, and he shook his head. "No. You don't remember much about life before prison, do you?"

"Not much. I was just in the way all the time, and my mother wanted to get rid of me. She ultimately did. I guess my father won't be sending me cards now. The prison system always forwarded them to me. I never replied, though."

"Because you don't know how to read or write." Dean scowled. "We'll change that, although I'm not sure I want those humans near you."

"Remember what I said about attentive

stallions being protective? This is an attentive stallion being protective. If you don't want him hovering, you'll have to tell him no."

"I'm used to telling people no using objects with excessive force. Does just saying no actually work?"

"Sometimes," Xena admitted. "Not always, though. So, if someone doesn't listen when you say no, fight back and request an angel to verify the truth. The court must abide by a self-defense request for angelic verification. That's your right, especially in a case where you used self-defense to protect yourself. If you're assaulted and take it to court, always request for an angel." Then, the woman heaved a sigh. "You didn't know you could request an angel, did you?"

"No."

"Dean?"

"What?"

"I think you should trot down to the courthouse in the morning and make certain that the judge knows that Layla wasn't aware of her rights."

"I think I shall do that, if you can keep an eye on her while I'm gone."

"I will feed her a cupcake for breakfast, and I think I'll have it laced with pixie dust. She'll have a good day. I'll get her a good grade. She'll want it after riding one of us—"

"She will ride me, if you please." Dean's

tone implied he'd fight his sister over it, and
Xena held her hands up in surrender. "Anyway, you're borderline too young to carry a
rider."

"Damn it."

"Her   weight   could   damage   your
spine. No."

Xena grumbled curses under her breath.

"How old does a unicorn need to be before being able to carry a rider?"

"Our species develops slowly. I couldn't
safely carry a rider until I turned twenty-five,
but I was ahead of the curve. As Xena's a
mare, she's a little slower on development.
She probably won't be able to carry a rider
until thirty-five to forty or so. We can live for
hundreds of years. Mom's almost a thousand."

Damn it. I hated new numbers. "I'm not
sure I understand what a thousand means."

"You're in your mid-twenties, so you've
lived about a quarter of a human's normal
lifetime." Dean selected an egg roll and held it
up, then he used a knife to cut it into four
pieces. Gesturing to one of the pieces, he said,
"This is what a quarter of an egg roll looks
like."

I regarded the three remaining pieces with
a frown. "I guess I've really spent a lot of time
in prison, haven't I?"

Dean grabbed three more egg rolls and
added them to his plate. "My oldest sister is

almost four hundred years old. So, this is how old she is if counted in egg rolls that represent roughly eighty years. We'll round up to a hundred since you know how hundreds work now."

"Compared to you, I'm going to die young, aren't I?"

"Not if I convert you into a unicorn. I promise you'll enjoy the process."

"I will?"

Xena reached over and smacked her brother. "No. You will not have sex with her so many times you convert her that way. There are other ways, one that doesn't potentially involve you repopulating the entire unicorn race through her on your own."

My eyes widened. "You can have sex with a woman so many times you can change her into a unicorn?"

"Yes. The mares can convert their man that way, too. Usually, people being converted drink a small amount of their partner's blood every day for a year or so. That is usually sufficient. And it won't work unless the person being converted genuinely wants it. But most conversions are successful, since unicorns won't convert anyone other than their life-long mate."

"Just so you're aware, an attentive stallion wanting to convert you would have to bed you just about every day for five or ten years to convert you into a unicorn that way. You'd probably have a ridiculous number of children before he finished the conversion process, and well, he'd probably want to be extra sure. You'd end up like our mother, with a foal constantly around. And my brother, fool like he is and too much like our father for your good, would enjoy it."

"Yes, I'll enjoy it, and I'll make sure she does, too," Dean announced.

Heaven help me. One unicorn wanted to take over the world, and the other had much naughtier ideas in mind. I reached over, claimed one of the egg rolls, and dipped it in the sauce before chewing on it, pondering the best way to tell the unicorns they were out of their minds. Before I could inform them of the truth, the waiter returned with the first of the dishes, covering every inch of free space. With so many new things to try, I abandoned my attempt to tell the unicorns they were crazy and went to work exploring the wonderful world of Chinese food.

I ATE enough for six people, only to discover Chinese food magically vanished from my stomach and left me hungry again after an hour. The hotel room, which had two beds, lacked any obvious ways for someone to feed themselves, and my stomach insisted it needed more food.

It kept growling at me.

"I'm not sure how this is going to work out," I admitted. I let them decide if I meant my cranky stomach or our sleeping arrangements.

"You take one bed; we'll take the other. Dean's used to having me latch onto him in the middle of the night. We unicorns like nap piles. The last time we had a family reunion, everyone decided to sleep on Dean, since Dad tossed him to the wolves."

"He took Mom on a date. That is not tossing me to the wolves. It's my fault I didn't run away like the rest of our brothers. Also, you and the rest of my sisters are not wolves. You're blood-sucking vultures."

"You're so mean to me, Dean."

"Just be happy Mom and Dad decided you were old enough to go off on your own."

"Conditionally. With you."

I needed to figure out how to contact Westin and kick his ass for abandoning me to the unicorns. I eyed the beds and their close proximity. "What are the odds of me waking up covered in unicorns?"

The siblings glanced at each other, and as one, they shrugged.

"Why am I hungry again? I just ate. I don't understand this."

"It's one of the marvels of the modern world. I'm always hungry again shortly after eating Chinese food, too," Xena admitted. "But it tastes so good, and then I feel hungry again, and then I get two dinners in one night, and there's nothing wrong with two dinners in one night."

"The only reason you get away with that is because you gallop around most of the time and burn off the calories. Layla can't burn off calories galloping around yet." Dean grabbed a black folder and flipped it open. "But as I, too, have mysteriously become hungry again, I shall order us pizza."

While rare, pizza did show up at the prison messes, and I'd enjoyed it the times I'd tried it. Usually, we got it when we were well behaved as a group, which happened once every blue moon according to the other inmates. "I like pepperoni."

"Well, that makes things easier. I'll just get extra pepperoni. You can live with that, Xena?"

"Get one with pineapple and fungus."

My eyes widened. "Fungus?"

"Mushrooms. My sister likes fungus and fruit on her pizza. Don't ask me why. I haven't figured that part out yet. She's a weird one, but I love her despite her oddities."

"You're one to talk. You scouted active

cases for someone interesting, and you requested to be pampered by a crazy person."

"Before you get upset over that, Beanie, she's totally right. I'm definitely crazy." I was certifiable for going along with two crazier unicorns—and liking it. The liking it part concerned me.

"That is a horrific nickname." Dean shuddered. "I'll beg, but please never call me that again."

"Clean? Sheen? Spleen? Dean the Spleen! Mean? Green?"

The stallion sighed. "Those are even worse than bean. Really, Layla? Spleen?"

"I feel my vocabulary is too limited right now."

"Queen," Xena suggested.

My eyes widened. "Dean the Clean Green Spleen Queen?"

"It somehow got even worse. I will order chicken wings, but please, no. My name is Dean. Without anything else attached."

"I will not encourage Layla to come up with something worse if you refrain from trying to seduce her while I'm around."

Dean pointed at the door. "Get out and get your own room."

"No. That does not mean you can evict me so you can continue your seduction plans. She is unavailable to be seduced."

I was? "This is not an invitation to be seduced or a rejection of any proposed seductions, but shouldn't I have a say in whether or not I'm seduced?"

"Well, she seems to have the important, practical life lessons learned." Xena pointed at me. "Listen to her. She has full say in whether or not she is seduced, and you're just going to have to wait until she gives you permission."

"I think you should go get your own room and leave me alone."

"No. If I leave the room, you will begin your seduction plans. You do not get to do such a thing. You're supposed to be my supervision, and I can't take over the world if you're busy seducing my sidekick."

"You can't have her. I saw her first."

"I don't care if you saw her first. She's more useful to my plans."

"How, exactly, is she more useful to your plans? My plans only involve her. I don't care about the rest of the world. If you want to take over the world, do so properly without using Layla, if you please!"

"I do not please."

I pointed at the menu. "Can one of you show me how to turn that into pizza, please? Also, I would appreciate if you showed me how to make that paper and my card turn into pizza. This seems like a very important form of magic."

Dean wrinkled his nose at his sister before

turning to me. "Ordering pizza is technology, not magic. To place an order, you use the phone or the internet. The menu, which you're pointing at, just tells you what the restaurant serves. Since we're at a hotel, and I didn't bring a laptop with me for this trip, we have to use the phone. I will call the restaurant, tell them where we are, what room we're in, and what we want to eat, and they will send over a driver. They'll bring a device that can read the card, and they will take the money they're owed for bringing us food. But I'll use my card for this, as it's my treat."

"But how did your card get money on it?"

"When I'm not crashing court sessions, I have a job."

"You do?"

"It is a very boring job, really. I'm on vacation."

"For the next six months? How did you get a vacation like that?"

"I asked for it."

"Who did you ask?"

"My boss."

"So, like the prison guards in charge of assignments?"

"Essentially, except I work because I need to earn money so I can spend money. In my case, my boss is also my father, and my job can be done anywhere in the world. But right now, Mom is doing my job for me. I'm hoping it will prevent the next sibling from coming around for a few extra months."

Xena clicked her tongue and shook her head. "He handles our parents' finances. He's the smartest of the males, and he likes stability. He'll be very attentive, but if I'm not allowed to try to take over the world, he's not allowed to be attentive."

"Before you two start arguing again, can you do a demonstration of how food is ordered on the phone? I feel this is an important life skill that may prevent me from stealing again."

Ordering seemed so much easier than stealing, even if I had to surrender the money from the card to receive my food.

"I'm not sure we're adult enough to teach a woman the ways of the world without creating an entity of pure evil," Xena admitted.

"With great power comes greater responsibility, and I'm going to misuse my great powers to teach her how to order pizza. Then I won't worry she'll be unable to feed herself should we be separated for any reason." Dean picked up the phone. "Okay, Layla. I'm going to teach you how to read some numbers. See this number on the paper?" He pointed at a string of numbers.

"I see them."

Dean tapped a button on the phone. "See the matching number on the buttons?"

"I do."

"Tap them in the same order as they're shown here."

I obeyed, taking care to make sure I hit them in the same order. When I pressed the last one, Dean held the phone to his ear. Within two minutes, he placed an order for three large pizzas, two bottles of soda, more chicken wings than I could count on two hands, and bread sticks.

"Thirty-six. Explain this number, please."

"Ten three times plus six is thirty-six. Three sets of ten is thirty. There are six wings more than thirty, which becomes thirty-six."

"That seems like such a random number. Why did you order that number of chicken wings?"

"I wasn't sure how many to get, they come in batches of twelve, so I decided I would order one for each of us."

Xena sighed. "I'm going to get fat, and this will be all your fault, Dean. When I get fat eating all this food, I will come for you."

"Will you, though? I'm sure you'll try, but once you're pleasantly plump, will you be able to catch me?"

With an infuriated shriek, Xena chased after her brother, and I amused myself watching the pair run around the hotel room.

SIX

One night with the unicorns had
driven me crazy.

SOMEHOW, I avoided sharing a bed with anyone, although I questioned how I'd gotten
onto the floor. I expected the soft bed had
something to do with my situation. The
prison beds—or cots, depending on how well
I'd behaved—tended to be rock hard. The
hotel mattress liked trying to eat unsuspecting people. Maybe it hadn't liked how I'd
tasted and spit me out.

Great. One night with the unicorns had
driven me crazy. Maybe crazier.

Oh, well.

The unicorns had fed me pizza, and upon
discovering how much I'd liked chicken
wings, Dean had given me his share, elevating
him to the best unicorn on Earth.

"Finally awake?" Xena bounced off the bed
and sat on the floor beside me. "You ate two
whole pizzas, every single chicken wing to

enter the room, and drank half a bottle of soda. I'm pretty sure you've never had much sugar before last night, because I've never seen a human bounce that much in my entire life. It was like watching a drunk, except you were hyper rather than drunk."

I struggled to remember last night, which had gone by in a food-filled blur. "Did that really happen?"

"Somewhat."

"Where's Dean?"

"Yelling at a judge, I expect. He's really good at yelling. He left an hour ago and told me to let you sleep as long as you needed. You slept right through him falling out of bed onto your little nest down there."

"I was wondering why I'm on the floor," I admitted.

"At around three in the morning, you went to the bathroom, and when you were finished, you staggered back in here, got somewhat confused, grabbed the nearest blanket, and curled up on the floor with it. You took Dean's blanket, by the way. Startled him awake, and then he added to your nest since he had no idea why you'd targeted his blanket, but he's an idiot stallion, so he wasn't going to take his blanket back. Really, he's just an idiot stallion. Don't mind him."

"I do have a bad habit of stealing things."

"Well, my brother has already come up

with various solutions to your blanket thievery. He is convinced if he purchases enough blankets, you will save him one. I believe he's already strategizing his blanket acquisitions. I'm concerned he's going to try to lure you to his bed through the use of soft blankets. Honestly, I won't blame you if you fall for that. Soft blankets are sinful, and if you have to accept a stallion to get a blanket, you could be worse off."

"I could be?"

"Sure. You wouldn't have the warm, soft blanket, but stallions are warm. I'm debating if I want to hunt a stallion or convert a human. Either way, I will win. My father, my brothers, and my sister's stallions are all heat generators. It's a selling point on why I should put up with a stallion."

"Let me guess. You want to steal your stallion because stealing is half the fun."

"That did not take you long to figure out at all. I'm so proud of you."

"I'm pretty sure the prison guards would call you a bad influence, Xena."

"Yes. I'm sure they would. And they would be correct. I do mean to take over the world. I don't mean to repopulate it with others of my kind, though. I'll leave that to my brothers, my parents, and my sisters. They all, for some damned reason, seem pretty keen on the idea."

"I would prefer to remain out of prison, so leave me out of any thefts for now."

"I appreciate you're considering participation in thefts later."

"It would have to be a really good theft."

"How about we steal one of your paintings?"

"What?"

"Well, someone had you painting really nice paintings, right? Probably counterfeits, from the sounds of it. Those paintings have to be somewhere. Let's go find out where one of them is and steal it."

"Why would we steal that? I can just paint a new one."

"You can do that. Actually, that's a really good idea. Let's go get you painting supplies while my brother is busy yelling at a judge. Dean'll feel better once he's done his duties as an overprotective stallion."

I doubted I would ever understand Xena, what went on in her head, or what drove her to want to take over the world when I thought she already had a good deal. Her brother obviously cared for her, she had a family who loved her enough to set limits, and she seemed happy. I wondered what life would've been like if I'd had a family who'd cared for me enough to stick around.

"Stealing one of your paintings would be a great entry into world domination. And I'd be

able to see one of your paintings. You said
you only did duplicates?"

"Not really. Sometimes I painted what I
was told, sometimes they told me to paint
something similar but not the same. It varied.
I'd work on a lot of paintings at one time, too.
The paint had to dry. They had an entire
room set aside for paintings. I spent most of
my time there."

"The room was probably dismantled the
instant the judge ordered the prison to be investigated. An undiscovered painting by a fa-
mous painter would be worth a fortune on
the market, and if your art was close enough
to pass, someone could age the paint and
canvas—assuming they used the same types
of canvas and methods they used in the era
the originals were painted. It's lucrative."

"How lucrative?"

"One painting could pay your rent and
cost of living for the rest of your life."

I was grateful she hadn't put a number to
that. "So, one of those is worth a lot, then."

"Yes, it's worth a lot. And if you're good
enough to create art that could pass as an
undiscovered piece, then it's worth the risk
keeping someone like you in the system. One
of those paintings, if successfully sold, could
keep numerous accomplices happy. How
many paintings have you finished? Wait. That
was a bad question. Can you tell me how

long it would take for you to finish a painting?"

"I'd finish six or seven paintings every few weeks, I suppose. The time between hearings."

"And you've been painting all of your life."

"Yeah."

"What awful people. I hope my brother stabs them, cooks them, and eats them."

"That's gross."

"Deserved, though."

"Would Dean actually eat them?"

"No. He prefers his meat incapable of speaking to him."

That worried me. "And you?"

"I'll try just about everything once."

"I will shank you with your own horn if you try to stab, cook, or eat me."

"You're very fond of shanking people."

Was I? I thought about that, and after consideration, I nodded. "It's effective at stopping people from doing things I don't want done to me. It is an efficient deterrent."

"I also like how you're somewhat uneducated, but you speak like you've been to school. Where did you learn phrases like efficient deterrent?"

"The prison guards, as they were constantly testing new deterrents to keep us in line. I didn't create many problems. I guess I was easily deterred."

"Unless someone got in your face, at which point, you would shank them."

"Exactly. I only shank someone when provoked. If they leave me alone, I will leave them alone."

"You're a walking deterrent."

"Am I?"

"Well, if I'd been there and seen you shank a bunch of people for bothering you, I wouldn't bother you. I'm a lot of things, but I'm not stupid. If you're the kind to wade in and shank people causing other people problems, I wouldn't bother anyone where you might catch me."

"I did do that sometimes."

"I know. We saw your file. Dean is quite the conspirator when he wants to be, and our species gives him a certain amount of leeway, especially when he expresses interest in someone of the other gender. Really, he was just bored and figured a woman from prison would be interesting. I'm still not sure how he convinced someone in the system he wanted some prison chick, though."

"I know some good psychologists in the prison system. Dean might benefit from them." I couldn't resent Dean for assuming someone involved with the prison system would be interesting. I certainly made court sessions interesting. "Why did he really decide to involve himself in my affairs?"

"He saw your picture and decided you were hot, you had to be interesting, and you'd keep him on his toes. It was lust at first sight, although that's not much considering we're talking about a stallion here. Lusty is their default."

"Is it?"

"Sadly, yes. But in good news, he finds you very attractive. Honestly, you seem rather plain to me, but I'm not the one who has to live with you. Well, mostly. Ugh. I don't want to think about my brother being lusty, but that's what I've been dealing with for weeks. Damn it. Let's go buy whatever it is you need to make paintings happen. Go take a bath and try not to drown yourself."

"You're going to have to explain that." After an entire evening of confessing my ignorance, it'd gotten easier to accept I knew jack shit about life outside of a small cell, no matter what the other inmates had discussed.

None of it had made a whole lot of sense to me, and I'd never trusted anyone enough to ask for explanations.

I'd gotten too much pity as it was when people learned I'd been a resident of the slammer for my entire life.

"Right. They have showers in prison, and you probably don't remember baths from before you were incarcerated. That's on me. Sorry. Let me introduce you to the wonderful world of bath pampering. You'll enjoy it. Just don't drown. I wouldn't want to explain to my brother how you drowned."

"A prisoner drowned once; a pipe had burst in a basement area, and nobody had bothered checking why the building's water was dribbling. Turns out it flooded that room, and he'd drowned before anyone figured it out."

"That sounds horrific."

"He was pretty horrific. Maximum security, in for life for some pretty brutal murders. He killed a couple of kids. The guards couldn't let him mingle with anyone because everybody wanted a round with him. I'd already figured out what my contribution would be."

"I'm almost afraid to ask, but I'm going to anyway. What would you have done?"

"I would've shanked him with a painting."

"I don't think you can shank anyone with a painting, Layla."

I snorted. "If you hit someone hard enough, anything can become a shank. The canvas frame could break if I failed to use enough blunt force to drive the entire thing into his person. Then I'd use my new shiv to carve a few lessons into him."

"Sometimes, I think you're utterly innocent, but then you inform me that you have considered shanking someone with a painting. Since that wasn't bad enough, should the canvas frame break, you'd transform your shank into a shiv and use it to carve messages onto another human being. I can't tell if you're innocent or possibly the handmaiden of the devil. I'm pretty sure anything blunt doesn't count as a shank, though. Aren't shanks typically something sharp?"

"In my world, as long as the job gets done, it's a shank. That's good enough for me. Do handmaidens of the devil get paid?"

"I like how you view that as a job opportunity."

"It seems important. I need to get paid to buy things. Nobody said anything about how I'd work to make the money I need to pay for things. I'm clear now on how money works enough to understand I have to earn money to spend it." All in all, I was proud of how quickly I'd grasped the concept once someone had explained it to me and taught me that the restaurant employees were paid to bring me food.

I still wasn't clear on how tips worked, but Dean had promised they'd be tipped well.

Xena laughed. "I have no idea if the devil is hiring, I'm afraid. Anyway, when you aren't contemplating how to murder someone with a blunt object, you seem pretty nice in general. If you need employment, I'm sure Dean would love to have you working for him. You'll have to rein him in, though. He'll pay you to be pretty for him. And as he's a stallion, he'll pay you to do nothing. You'd be bored out of your mind within a few hours. So, make sure if he's going to pay you, he gives you meaningful work. Painting is meaningful, but he'd want you to paint things you like. He'd probably even start helping you sell your art if that's what you like. But be careful of my brother; stallions are tricky."

If I ignored her brother, I bet I'd drive him insane. Driving the stallion insane would keep me amused, and I'd happily accept his money while doing it. "I can be a nice person and shank people who deserve it, right? That's something I can do outside of prison, right?"

"Self-defense is legal, but you'd definitely want to use an angel to verify you did it out of self-defense."

"Should I just ask for an angel every time I get on the wrong side of the law?"

"While the court would not appreciate the bill for that, it's not a bad idea. With your luck, it's a really good idea, actually."

"Okay. Have I done anything yet that might land me back in prison?"

"I like that you automatically assume you're going to do something that will land you back into prison."

"Well, I've met myself. I always land back into prison."

"Only because you were being used for your artistic ability. That's not your fault. But I suppose I do need to teach you how to stay out of prison. You aren't the kind to be happy living in ignorance, are you?"

"I've done that enough already. Can we start with the painting supplies?"

"Miss painting already?"

I shrugged. "I'm good at it."

"Right. Sure. Let's go buy you some painting supplies. But first, I'll show you the wonders of a nice bath. This one is a luxury bath, too. It has jets, and I don't know a single woman who doesn't like the jets. Dean called around until he found a hotel with a jet tub, as he thought you'd like to indulge. Of course, he didn't really anticipate you having no idea what a bath is, but that's all right. I didn't anticipate that either. Things will be different now, that much I can promise."

"But will they be better?"

"Yes. You'll see. Just don't ask Dean that question. He'll twist himself into a pretzel trying to prove life is better with him around. And that life is better, period. Actually, ignore me. Ask Dean that question. You deserve a good stallion pampering you, and you've passed all of my tests."

"I have?"

"Layla, you shared your first cupcake without anyone suggesting you should. You personify innocence right up until you tell me you want to shank somebody. Then you're aware of the realities of the world without really understanding the world you live in. You could teach angels a thing or two about what it means to be pure in spirit. How they cultivated that in a prison, I don't know, but I won't see that ruined. And although my brother can be obnoxious, he will take care of you, assuming you let him. That will be an entirely different problem, but one he'll be happy to have, so don't you worry about that. For now, worry about enjoying your bath and think about what art supplies you need to paint what you like."

I could do that. I hoped.

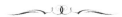

YEARS OF DODGING unwanted attention in prison gave me an edge in identifying creeps, but I hadn't expected two white men in suits to make a run at me while I walked with Xena. To keep men's filthy mitts off me, I'd learned to act before I thought, and I had jammed my knee in my first assailant's groin before I registered they were targeting me in the first place.

As a knee to the groin wouldn't necessarily keep a man down, I grabbed the nearest object I might use as a weapon.

I'd never tried to shank somebody with a purse before, but Xena's had good heft, and I smacked it into the asshole's head as hard as I could. It took five solid blows to knock him to the concrete.

"Here. Use this." Xena held out an empty plastic bottle.

I ignored her, secured my grip on the straps of her purse, and debated how to beat the second man.

He dove behind the wheel of a black car, and his groaning accomplice scrambled to catch up, crawling into the back. The vehicle took off with the back door still open. To my disappointment, the battered asshole somehow stayed inside rather than falling out and being tenderized on the asphalt.

I gave Xena her purse back. "Thank you for loaning me that."

"You're welcome. That was a very effective use of your knee. His friend grabbed his crotch in sympathy. And whimpered. I think you relocated his testicles into his skull with that hit. Was beating him with my purse necessary?"

"Yes. He hadn't gone down with the first hit. Always be sure of your opponent. If they aren't on the ground writhing and crying, you're not done with the beating."

"I shouldn't be surprised, but I am. Okay. This presents several problems."

"It does?"

"Well, two well-dressed men just tried to kidnap you, Layla. That's a problem."

"But they didn't."

"While that's true, they still tried, and that is a problem. It's going to be an even bigger problem when my brother finds out. He'll go ballistic."

"Math is not my strong point, but even I know several is more than one, and that's one problem."

Xena sighed. "You exist to vex me, don't you?"

"That seems like a reasonable assumption."

She sighed again, longer and louder. "Someone was waiting for you, knew where you'd be, and tried to kidnap you. That's three problems."

"Okay."

"You don't care, do you?"

I shrugged. "Your purse made a good weapon. Can I borrow it again if someone tries something like that again?"

"Sure. That said, I think I'm going to buy you a knife. Or a gun. Or a billy club."

"The prison guards really do not like when the inmates get a hold of any of those three things."

"You're not an inmate anymore. I can't get you a gun since you're not licensed, but I can get you a knife."

"Can it be a painting knife?"

"There are painting knives?"

"I can show you, if you show me where painting things can be purchased. Does my card have enough to buy painting supplies?"

"Yes. There's plenty on your card for painting supplies. I'll help you with the math in the store. We'll get a little notebook before we go in, and I'll teach you how to do math that way. It'll kill time while my brother deals with a judge and attorneys. Honestly, I think it'll take him all day. We have a slight edge in our species, but—"

A phone rang in Xena's purse, and the woman dug into the bag to retrieve it. She tapped on the screen and held it to her ear. "Hello? Oh. Dean. Yes, she's fine. We're going to an art store. Everything's fine. Okay. Sure. I expect we'll be at the art store for several hours. We're going to either need a driver, or you're going to have to take your lazy ass to the driver's place and do that stupid test to get a license that's valid on this continent."

That caught my attention. "Dean has a license that's not valid on this continent?"

"He was originally licensed to drive in Africa, and well, they don't really have set rules in that part of the world, so the United

States doesn't like allowing people holding that license to drive on their roads. It leads to accidents. But Dean can drive. And he does a good job. He's never had an accident. He got a lot of practice in Germany with Mom and Dad."

I stared at her.

"Dean, just ask the damned judge to get you a license so we can get a vehicle and drive her. You can make those arrangements. Buy a damned car while you're at it. You can afford it. It won't take long to get your licensing issue sorted out. You know how to drive, so stop being a pain in my ass. I know you're a beautiful stallion and the world should admire you, but Layla needs her art supplies, and if I can't carry a human, I certainly can't carry her art supplies. I'm planning on turning her loose. She might buy half the store. No, we are not buying a herd of horses so they can carry her stuff. If you get stallions, you'll get jealous if they like Layla and pissed if they even look at me. You cringe like a wuss around the geldings for some reason, and you hate having to establish to the mares you're not available for their entertainment. No. That's final. No horses. Get your damned license like the adult you are. We have those damned species exemptions, so make use of them. I'd get mine, but you bastards won't let me learn how to drive until I'm able to carry someone. And that, for the record, is ridiculous."

Xena hung up, growled curses, and shoved her phone back into her purse. "Stupid pig-headed brother!"

"Who is 'you bastards?'"

"My parents, my brothers, and my older sisters. They seem to think unless I'm mature enough to carry a ride, I'm not mature enough to drive a car. Ridiculous. I'm the only damned woman my age who can't drive."

"Except for me?"

"Well, okay. There are now two of us. It's so damned frustrating!"

"Why doesn't Dean have a license, then?"

"He's a sentimental idiot and feels bad I don't have a license yet. Actually, I think he's avoided it because he's incapable of telling me no."

Having seen Dean tell Xena no multiple times since meeting them, I raised a brow.

"About things like giving me lessons on how to drive a car. He feels guilty."

"You two are really crazy, aren't you?"

"That's funny, coming from a chick who just kneed a man in the groin and beat him into submission with my purse."

"If he hadn't gotten into my space, I wouldn't have beaten him."

"You know what? Let's get out of here before someone calls the cops. Shopping is so much better than dealing with the cops."

I didn't have to think on that one long. "Let's get out of here."

XENA TOOK me to store after store to prepare me for life as a free woman. First, she took me to a clothing store, subjecting me to several hours of trying on new clothes. Then, as our purchases took five large bags to carry, we returned to the hotel to drop them off before heading to a store that sold phones like hers. The resulting argument amused me. As I didn't have an address or an identification card, the store didn't want to sell me a phone. Xena ultimately added me as a user on her account and got me a phone that way.

Given five or ten minutes, I expected she would've tried to shank the store employee with her phone.

I questioned the whole phone thing, as I had no idea how to use the damned thing. It went into a purse Xena had picked for me, promising I'd like the purse due to the problem of pockets in women's pants. It didn't take me long to realize what she meant.

A few pairs of pants she'd made me purchase had pockets, including the one she'd suggested I wear for the rest of our shopping outage.

Xena saved the art store for last, and the vast quantity of supplies froze me in the entry. Canvases of all sizes waited for me to claim them as mine. Some came primed, some didn't, and I could do whatever I wanted with them. Xena fetched a cart, and patted it. "To keep things somewhat reasonable, let's try to limit your purchases to what will fit in this."

Considering I wanted every canvas in the store, I foresaw a serious problem in my immediate future. "I don't like that rule."

"I bet you don't. Start with the paints, brushes, and whatever else it is you need to paint with, then you can fill the rest of the cart with canvases. If you put the canvases in first, you'll have to put some back to get the basics." Xena pointed at a sign hanging from the ceiling. "Paints are that way. What type do you use?"

"Oil."

"Of course. You'd have to, if they're trying to use your artwork to create counterfeits. This way!" Xena pushed the cart towards the sign, navigating through a sea of art supplies, sketching supplies, and racks upon racks of markers and other toys I wanted to play with. I'd used markers and sketch books to plan paintings before, and I snagged Xena's arm, pointing at them.

"What is it?"

"I want those."

"Okay." Xena backed up until we stood together, regarding the boggling collection of markers. "You know what? Pick the most expensive markers in all the colors you need. I'll call Dean and tell him he should get his ass over here and pay for it. He likes saying it's his job as a stallion to provide for his mare, so he better start providing."

"Do I have enough money to buy them?"

"Layla, you could probably buy everything in the store and have money left over. If you exceed how much you have, or even get close, I'll tell you. But you could buy every color—" Xena squinted, bent over, and pointed at something stashed beneath the individual markers. "That set has two hundred colors. Buy that. It's cheaper per marker that way, and it's the expensive brand. I'm assuming the expensive brand will be good."

I found the box and pulled it out from the shelf. It took up a lot of space in the cart, and I frowned.

"Don't worry about the cart rule. It was a stupid rule anyway. Just keep it to two carts. That'll fit in whatever the hell vehicle Dean picks up."

"Dean is going to get mad at us, isn't he?"

"He'll stop being angry the instant he sees how happy you are with your new art supplies. Just look really happy when you're unwrapping everything. That's how stallions roll. It'll give him something to do, anyway. It's easy to get lazy when you're old and bored. So, funding your art supplies will keep him motivated."

"Being a unicorn sounds like hard work."

"Ain't that the truth. We have to run around in our human form most of the time, since people freak out if they see a unicorn. Can you imagine it? My family is as mixed as it gets. I'm African, my brother's Greek, my mother's something-or-other. Actually, Mom doesn't talk about it, because her people don't actually exist anymore. Dad looks African, but he's actually early Roman."

"Early Roman?"

"Yeah. Dad's old. Mom isn't his first mare. His first mare died a long time ago. But most people were dark-skinned unless from a northern clime, and the northerners had a rough time of it. Dad's darker than Dean, lighter than me, but he looks more like Dean than I do in build and facial structure. Just don't get Dad started. He'll start yelling in Latin, Greek, or some other old language. It's fun when he starts up in Spanish, since his form of Spanish is from when it was first being developed, so nobody who speaks modern Spanish can understand him. If he gets really upset, he'll start up in Aramaic. It's part of what we are. Once we hear a language, we can learn to speak it. It's magic. You'll develop it should my brother successfully convert you. And the converted keep their original magical abilities, too."

"I don't have any magic."

Xena snorted, and she checked the box of my markers before checking over the racks. She grabbed a few extra markers and tossed them into the cart, before adding several large sketching pads. "You've been told you don't have magic because someone without magic is easier to control and imprison than someone with magic. If the goal was to keep you under their thumb, you probably have some form of ability but were never tested. Ignorance is a good way to keep untrained magic under control if there's no conditions for the magic to grow or be used."

Huh. "I hadn't thought about that."

"That's exactly what they want." Xena narrowed her eyes while regarding my acquisitions. "Okay. You're covered on markers. If you're going to be coloring with markers, you're going to need sketching pencils and that kind of stuff. That's over here. We'll grab the most expensive set they have and hope that's good enough, plus sharpeners and whatever else you might need."

I had done sketching with pencils, and I recognized one of the brands as something I'd been given to use. I pointed at them. "I've used those."

"And that would be the most expensive set of the lot. They weren't joking about cultivating your artistic ability. Damn. Can't make masterpieces without good base supplies, I guess. Oh, well. Dean will pay it, especially when it makes you happy." Xena added the pencils and more sketch books to the cart. "Onto the paints. Point at the brands you know, and we'll go from there."

A dizzying selection of oil paints waited for me, and nothing resembled the tubes I'd used. I shook my head. "I guess they weren't a brand."

"Or they hid the brand. They could have been hand mixed to get the formulas right. They sell the pigments so you can make your own paints."

"I don't know how to do it."

"Well, going with the most expensive has worked so far, so we'll do that. And you don't need to match pigment types with original paintings for this. Modern paints will do what you need, and if the quality isn't what you want, I guess we can look into mixing your own. Dean will just love having to supply you with everything you need to do that."

Judging from her tone, Dean would hate everything about it. "What happened to us using the notebook to do the math?"

"I didn't realize how much stuff we'd be buying. We'll do the math at the hotel when we're going over everything. That's close enough."

While I lacked a good grasp of life outside of prison, I could understand why Dean would want to keep a close eye on his younger sister. In his shoes, I'd be wary about leaving her unsupervised.

Xena's phone rang, and she dug for the device while I raided the paint supplies, grabbing a bulk set of colors and filling in the blanks for what I'd need, while also buying extra tubes of the colors I'd use more often.

"Hi, Dean. Did you get a vehicle? We're going to need it. Layla is rampaging through the art store, and she's currently buying ten tubes of white paint for some reason. No, wait. Even more. That's a lot of white paint."

To screw with her, I picked up a few extra tubes of white to add to the cart. I found large tubs of primer, which also went into the cart along with various types of clear coats.

"Huh. I think she can read when there is paint involved. She's examining the labels and figuring it out without much difficulty, so maybe she has some preliminary reading skills."

I picked up the primer and pointed at the word. "I do know this one. Actually, I know a lot of these words because we'd talk about them during my assignments, and I learned to associate them with the word. That counts as reading?"

"Close enough. Yes, Dean. That's the store we're at. We're both going to need to be fed. Shopping is hard work. Also, she has clothes, but I don't think we have enough suitcases and bags. I took care of the other mandatory items a woman needs to survive in the world. So, after we're done in the art store, we should be set."

After I got all the colors I wanted into the cart, I rampaged through the brushes. The variety baffled me, but I discovered I could identify the type of brush I liked by touch. I got them in all shapes and sizes, looking forward to experimenting with some I hadn't seen before. Cups and palettes went into the cart next, along with a paintbrush organizer, several easels, and a few aprons that might save my clothing from the paints. Then I grabbed several large tins of paint thinner and shoved them on the bottom rack of the cart.

I had no idea where I'd put the canvases, so I stared at Xena.

"I need to get off the phone, Dean. Layla's filled the cart, and she's looking at me. She has a very unhappy expression, probably because she can't fit her canvases in the cart. I told you we'd do two carts, Layla. We'll get canvases, don't worry. Ah, sorry. I didn't want Layla to shank me with one of her new paintbrushes. Can you be here in thirty minutes? That'll give her some time to explore after she loads a cart with canvases. Okay. Drive safe." Xena tossed her phone into her purse. "He's mad that I made him do so much, but he has a license and an SUV. He complained that they made him take the actual driver's tests, but they didn't make him wait for appointments, at least. He passed with a perfect score, which he's very proud of. He's going to come here after he picks up a few suitcases."

"He should get a cupcake for doing a good job."

"We can make him drive us to a bakery. They'll have cupcakes. There won't be pixie dust ones unless we go to a licensed bakery, but there are a lot of really good baked goods you can try. You might be overwhelmed with the selection, though."

"One of each isn't possible?"

"Only if you want to make yourself very, very sick."

Well, that was disappointing. "I guess I don't need to get too many canvases if there's other places I can buy them?"

"There are. We can even order them online if you want."

I'd heard about online ordering while in prison, but how it worked remained a mystery—one I wanted to solve. "How many canvases should I get?"

"Let's get at least twenty. I expect you'll be doing a lot of painting as a coping mechanism. If we get panels, we can get you a lot without them taking up a lot of space." Xena returned to the entry of the store, where the carts and canvases waited. "Grab a cart, load it up. Go to town. We'll make it fit in the SUV one way or another."

Unicorns existed to confuse me, but I took a cart from the line and obeyed, starting with larger canvases like the ones I'd worked on in prison before discovering the flat panels I could buy in large packs. By the time Dean arrived, the store and its vast selection overwhelmed me to the point I wanted to leave to escape it.

Dean's brows rose when he looked over the carts. "Well, that should keep you busy for a while. Let's get this checked out. Did you make her do all the math for that, Xena?"

"While I'm planning on being a dictator, I'm not evil. No. I'll go over the receipt with her and make her do the math once we're settled for the night. It'll be a good, practical exercise. I'll also start her reading and writing with her art supplies."

"Or you could let her paint for a while without us bothering her," Dean suggested.

"Who are you and what have you done with my brother?"

"I spent half of my day arguing with a judge, an attorney, and an angel. Two angels, since I annoyed the first so much she called in a reinforcement."

"You didn't."

"I only partially contributed to the angel calling for reinforcements, but yeah. It went that well. I have a briefcase full of paperwork I need to review with Layla, but that can wait until tomorrow. I had a chance to have a long talk with one of the prison guards."

"Talk implies you were rational and calm during the discussion."

"I was. Mostly. I only left a few hoof prints in the wall on either side of his head to impress upon him it was unwise to trifle with me."

"How much of the talking did you do as a unicorn?"

"Only enough to convince him screwing around with me would be a very poor idea, and to prove my species was as I claimed."

"Please tell me that's the extent of it."

"Mostly."

"Damn it, Dean!"

"What? I don't like how they treated Layla."

Xena sighed, and as I expected the siblings would start fighting in earnest, I returned to browsing the selection of goods, discovering another row of easels I'd missed before, larger and much nicer than the ones I'd found in boxes and put in the cart. "Xena, look at these easels."

The woman joined me, and she whistled. "You should get one."

"I should?"

She pointed at one that stood at eye level. "That one, for your main projects. The other ones you got are table easels, and they aren't all that tall. That one looks really nice. Dean, tell your mare she should get this easel."

Dean joined us, and he looked the easels over, checking the price tags. He pointed at one with a rich red wood. "This one is probably better, judging from its price tag."

"Are we just buying everything that's most expensive in the store and assuming it's better?"

"Yes," they replied.

Xena turned and skipped off. "I'll find an employee to see if there's a box or something."

"I bought too much," I confessed, looking over both carts with dismay. "I don't even know how much I've spent, but I've spent too much."

"You haven't spent anything because I'm buying it all. Consider it a Christmas present."

"A what present?"

Dean sighed. "Christmas. It's a holiday. I'm guessing you were incarcerated at a secular prison, then."

"A what?"

"Secular means non-religious. Christmas is a religious holiday. Mostly, people just give each other presents and celebrate being with their family. Unicorns aren't part of the Christian pantheon, but we enjoy it anyway. We went to a Christian church once as a family. Apparently, some Christians don't believe in unicorns, and nothing tests their beliefs more than an entire herd of unicorns listening to the sermon while sniffing the poinsettias. We may have eaten a few. We had a great time, although that one little old lady was convinced we were demons in disguise."

"You're not?"

"No, we aren't demons in disguise."

"Are you sure this isn't too much?"

"I'm sure. You can tell me all about what you bought and why when we get to the hotel room."

With wide eyes, I stared at both carts. If I

tried to teach him about everything, we'd be up all night. "That's a lot of explaining."

"And you're worth the effort, so I'm happy to listen to you. But first, let's get all of these purchased and into the SUV. There is an important matter we do need to discuss back at the hotel, but then you'll have my undivided attention. I want to know about your painting, because from everything I know about you, it's an important part of who you are."

"I got markers, too."

"Markers are fun, but all I use them for is coloring books," Dean admitted. "I'm still guilty of getting crayons and playing in coloring books."

"You do what with what in what?"

"And there's my addition to today's purchases. Obviously, it's time someone introduced you to the glorious world of crayons and coloring books," Dean announced, turning around and marching across the store. "Wait here for Xena. I'll be right back. Actually, no. If you see something you want, put it in the cart. If it doesn't fit in the cart, just get another cart."

Unicorns existed to confuse me. Of that, I was certain.

SEVEN

I need you to pose for me.

THE ART SUPPLIES barely fit into the large SUV Dean had acquired, and the challenge pleased both unicorns, who wasted an entire hour strategizing how to avoid making two trips. The easels created the most problems, as the ones I liked couldn't be unassembled without tools and a lot of effort. My suggestion to tie them to the roof was met with disdained snorts from the siblings.

As I had no idea how to drive the vehicle, I kept my desire to tie them to the roof to myself.

At the hotel, Xena demanded I stay in the room and sort my acquisitions while they handled ferrying everything. To make sure I stayed put, she gave me the markers, pencils, and my largest sketchbook, pointed at the couch, and suggested I start planning my next painting. I figured she wanted to make sure nobody tried to make a mess of the evening by attempting to grab me out of the parking lot.

While rare, painting without guidance did happen in prison, although I'd never found out what had happened to my woodland scenes, all of which classified as figments of my imagination. I'd seen a few forests before from the window of the prison bus, but I'd never stepped foot into one.

Even in prison, I'd heard of unicorns, but the reality of them went against the whispered talk of pure beings. Instead of pure innocence, they brought chaos with them, turning my life upside down. While an almost boring white and gray, they'd colored my world in unexpected ways.

I'd paint them both, and they'd bring color to nature in their wake. I'd painted few winter scenes, but I liked the idea of the cold making way to them. I waited for them to bring everything to the room, and to fill the time, I sketched the basic outlines I'd use as a guide when painting.

On the third trip, I considered the siblings, and I pointed at Dean with my pencil. "I need you to pose for me."

"What about me?" Xena whined.

"You get to pose for me after I'm finished with him."

"You're doing this as revenge for the clothing shopping, aren't you?"

"No. It's revenge for not having enough space in the SUV to go to the bakery you promised."

"Crap. I forgot about the bakery. Okay. That's fair. I'll empty the SUV while you have your way with my brother. Then we'll talk him into taking us to the bakery."

"Is there are reason we can't order in baked goods?" Dean asked.

"Yes. She's never been in a bakery before as a customer. She needs to pick her treats in person."

"Can you accept a trip to the bakery tomorrow, Layla? I'll order in some baked goods tonight. I'll explain why after you're done sketching me and my sister. It involves the paperwork I got from the courthouse."

"Yes, I'm okay with that. I don't have to go to a bakery right away. I would like to see a bakery, however."

"Then it's decided. Sorry, Xena. Can you handle the easels alone?"

"I am a strong, beautiful woman. I can handle anything! It will just take me a few trips to get the rest is all." Xena strolled out of the room and closed the door behind her.

"How are we going to fit everything into the SUV tomorrow? There's clothes we have to deal with, too."

"Easy. Xena will run while I drive."

My eyes widened. "But cars go really fast."

"We're just as fast, and she could use the exercise. It'll be okay. We'll get rid of excess packaging and make it fit. We only have a two-hour drive to get to where we'll be staying for a while. I think I can make everything fit without making her run, though."

"But she can keep up?"

"She really can. I've clocked her at sixty, and she can maintain that for an hour before she needs a breather. She'll be fine. I'm more worried about you. There was definitely a counterfeit art ring running out of the prisons, and you were their star painter. They'll do a lot to get you back or silence you to prevent you from revealing their schemes."

All telling Dean about the two men in suits would do was worry him, so I decided to keep my mouth shut about the incident. "But you were able to question someone?"

"A prison guard who failed to get out of work in time to run once word hit the wire that the ring had been exposed. He hadn't wanted to talk, but I convinced him."

With force, something I didn't mind at all. "Okay. You'll tell me more after I finish sketching you?"

"Of course. I will protect you."

"I can protect myself."

"And I will protect you in such a way you will never have to worry about going to prison ever again."

Under no circumstances could I tell him about my altercation with the men in suits, as it would take an angel to keep me out of prison after assaulting the one. "Become a unicorn. I want to paint you."

I'd take my time with him, too. I needed to think about what I would do with a unicorn so determined to protect me from myself.

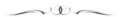

DRAWING DEAN CHALLENGED ME. Between his curves and the way he carried himself, pride etched into every line, it took me several hours to sketch him to my satisfaction. Xena regarded my work with a mix of fascination and horror.

"I have to go next?" she whispered, her eyes wide.

"I'm sure you'll be fine. You only have to stand still for a while. And move when I tell you to. It's not hard."

Xena pointed at her brother. "He's going to be frozen in that position forever."

Both of Dean's delicate ears turned back.

"Put those ears back where they belong, Mr. Dean," I ordered, pointing my pencil at him. "I'm not done with you yet!"

I'd finished his ears long ago, but I enjoyed bossing the stallion around. I could understand why people liked being obeyed.

Power tasted sweet, even if I used it for something as little as making a unicorn stand still for a while.

Dean snorted, but he turned his ears forward.

"I'm telling Mom and Dad you're whipped by a convict."

I laughed. "I haven't whipped him. I slapped his ass once. He can jump pretty high."

"Well, you startled him."

"Nobody expects to be slapped on the ass in court." I checked my sketch, added a few finishing touches, and gave a satisfied nod. "Okay. You're done, Dean." I thought I was going to use two unicorns in my painting, but I decided I liked the balance with only one. "You're off the hook for the moment, Xena. I'll paint him first, and I'll do one of you later."

"Hah. You're a most benevolent dictator. I will have to put you in charge of countries I like when I take over the world. A proper world ruler always keeps a few benevolent dictators around."

I turned the sketch so Xena could see it. "The paper wasn't big enough for you and your brother's ego. You just wouldn't fit."

"Okay. I'm going to go out on a limb here and say, just from your drawing skills, there's a damned good reason that art counterfeiting ring wanted to keep you in prison working for them. You could sell the sketch and make good money."

I looked at the sketch, which had gone from a basic outline to shaded and defined, which would make painting from it both easier and harder. "I meant to do a basic sketch, but he kept standing there, and I kept drawing."

Dean heaved a sigh, and he transformed into his human form with a faint pop. "And since you were enjoying yourself, I couldn't really justify asking you to stop drawing. If this is what the rest of my life is going to look like, can I request no more than an hour a session? I like moving."

"Ten-minute breaks to trot around between sessions?"

"I can work with that."

"I can do that." I set aside my sketchbook and stretched my hands. "That did take longer than I thought it would. I'm sorry. What happened this morning with the judge?"

"Chaos. All but one of the guards had bailed, and I'm guessing the police only nabbed the one by good fortune; they'd caught him leaving the night shift, so he'd missed the warning the ring had been busted. Once he started talking, the judge and angels got a list of names of those involved. Their information dried up at one of the sellers. We got a confirmation that they were using you to paint 'newly discovered' pieces of art to sell to private buyers and museums. What we don't understand is how they were bypassing the counterfeit checks. The paints they used then aren't the same as they use now, and some of the pigments don't even exist anymore."

"They used special paint; she couldn't find any of the paints she was used to, although I think they were using some modern primers; she recognized the primers and coats, and she had some knowledge of written colors. So, they were labeling the colors and she could read those labels, but they weren't anything mass produced. The store had a good selection of brands."

Dean shook his head, retrieved a briefcase from near the door, and sat on the couch beside me. "Their plan was brilliant, really. They kept you just ignorant enough you had no idea you were part of a very illegal and profitable art counterfeiting ring. The lawyers and judges getting a share of the profits made sure they didn't ask questions that would reveal your activities. The change of judge for your latest trial sank them—as did your defense attorney, too new to have been initiated into the ring. Our guess is they were going to wait until she was struggling to draw her in.

They had someone inside the court system who handled the scheduling make sure your case was given to judges who would send you back to prison, no matter what crime you committed."

I shrugged, as there wasn't a whole lot I could say.

"It's not your fault, Layla. Your life was very carefully orchestrated from the moment a greedy prison supervisor realized you're artistically talented." Dean glanced at my sketchbook. "More than just talented. Talented and practiced. You've been spending your entire life drawing and painting, and the result is someone who can produce art equal to the masters. Someone likely used magic to age the paint and canvas so they'd pass as the real deal. Assuming you enjoy painting, you don't need to go to college. You just need a basic education, and we can teach you when you're not painting. And if you're tired of painting, we can look into other options for you. You don't need to keep painting unless you want to."

"I like to paint."

"And draw, as you've been happily sketching for hours." Dean set his briefcase on the coffee table and opened it. "I was given a list of people to be wary of along with their photographs. If you see any of these people, you should be very careful, as they're confirmed to be part of the counterfeiting ring. At this point, kidnapping is more likely than murder, but I'd rather take no chances at all."

Dean lifted out several sheets of paper with rows of pictures on them featuring men and women, some of whom I recognized as prison guards and other workers in the legal system. I pointed at one of the prosecuting attorneys. "This is the guy who likes to blame women for being raped."

"Yeah. Judge Davids had opinions about that one. He's facing a lot of charges now for concocting false accusations while knowing they were false. He's also going to be charged with his participation in the ring. I expect he'll be in the first batch to face justice for his crimes. He's already facing debarring."

"Facing what?"

"He's having his law license revoked for participating in a felony. They're revoking it until his trial as a precaution. All the attorneys on this list are facing that."

"But why do you know that?"

"I happened to be in the room when the judge placed the calls to the bar association with the charges. Apparently, North Carolina has taken a more aggressive stance about attorneys and felonies. It's harder to have a law license revoked elsewhere, or so Judge Davids explained."

I put a check mark on the images of people I knew.

Xena snorted and pointed at the white men in suits I'd tangoed with before our shopping expedition. "I wasn't going to mention this before, but these two had it out for Layla this morning. She educated them. This charming fellow got a knee to his groin and beaten into submission with my purse. Those things that she told you about trying to turn blunt objects into shanks or shivs? They're true. I thought she might actually transform my purse into a piercing weapon by the time they bailed. It took her all of five seconds to subdue the one. I'm actually impressed they both left; the guy she'd beaten had to crawl into their car."

Dean grunted. "Why didn't you tell me this earlier? By earlier, I mean when it happened."

"She was fine, I wasn't worried about her ability to take care of herself, and you were busy. And since no cops showed up, we went about our day. Who are they?"

Dean rummaged through his briefcase, referenced the number beside their pictures, and said, "Camdenno and Larenzo Manetti. They're brothers and former drug runners who seem to have moved into black market art. According to their biography, they act refined and cultured, luring people in by pretending they're reformed and showcasing how former thugs can be valuable members of society. In good news, the note on their file marks them both as general pacifists; that's what drove them out of drug running in the first place. They preferred ensnaring their victims with honey and addictives rather than violence. Kidnapping is borderline for them, at least according to this."

"So, are you saying I should have hit him harder or been easier on him?"

Both unicorns bowed their heads and sighed.

"What? I thought it was a good question."

"I'm going to answer with harder," Dean replied.

"Just make sure you request an angel's verification of self-defense immediately if approached by the police. And if an angel isn't summoned, refuse to acknowledge them beyond demanding an angel to verify the truth. That's important." Xena grabbed the briefcase and sorted through the pages. "Damn. There are a lot of nasty people in this file, Dean. I think we should clean house."

"No."

"Don't be rude. If we clean house, we'd be doing North Carolina a favor, and we'd be protecting Layla at the same time."

"That's not how this works, Xena."

"It should be. It would be showing off my qualifications to rule the world."

"No, Xena."

"I don't agree with you. We should. You do want to protect Layla, don't you? Solving the problem in its entirety protects her."

"We don't have the legal authorization to launch such a campaign and doing so might land Layla in jail. Again. So, the answer is no."

"It would only be a problem if we got caught. The whole idea is to avoid being caught."

"No."

"I don't like that word, and I'm formally requesting that you remove it from your dictionary."

"The answer is still no, Xena."

"We have to do something."

"We will do something, but that something is not take on an entire counterfeiting ring on our own."

"That's nonsense. We'd just have to call in the family, and we'd be done within a week. Then we could introduce your little lady here to Mom and Dad."

"That's not how this works, Xena. First, Layla does get a say in this. Second, bringing Mom and Dad here would be a disaster. Third, if we brought the entire family here, they wouldn't break down the counterfeiting ring. They'd take it over, and then they'd reform it into a new art market specifically for profit purposes."

"But Layla would be paid her fair share of the profits, and they'd buy back the counterfeits at cost so the victims wouldn't be hurt from the ring. After that's sorted, they'd showcase the counterfeits to show off Layla's skills at painting and resell the original works as pieces inspired by the classical artists."

With a frown, Dean considered his sister.

No wonder the woman wanted to take over the world. Given a chance, she might get away with it.

"Question."

Dean and Xena disengaged from their staring match to give me their attention.

"Will your family pose, too?"

Xena giggled. "I bet we could talk them into it. By talk, I mean, Dean would get offended if they upset you, so all you'd have to do to get the entire herd to pose for you is bite your lip and look sad. Stallions get really upset when their lady of choice is unhappy for any reason."

"Dean, you need to grow a backbone and possibly see a doctor if you're that easily manipulated."

Dean glared at me. "That's not how it works. Stallions are supposed to care about their lady's happiness. We're supposed to treat women well."

"I think she's trying to say that you shouldn't be walked on. She's spent her entire life making sure nobody walks on her, so it makes sense it goes against her general nature to walk on others." Laughing, Xena resumed going through the paperwork. "I bet the family could put an end to this mess without breaking any laws. I still want to stage a museum heist to get back one of Layla's paintings, though."

"No."

"Come on. I bet we could pull that off legally, too."

"You can't legally steal something from a museum, Xena. It's not possible."

"Can, too."

"Cannot."

"Can, too."

"Cannot."

I held up my hand. "If either one of you say another word without answering one of my questions, you're buying me more chicken wings for dinner tonight."

Dean smirked. "How many chicken wings would you like?"

Why had I agreed to cooperate with the damned unicorns? Sighing, I shook my head. "Xena, this question is for you. Why do you think we could rob a museum legally?"

"If I approach the museum about testing their security team, explain the situation, and pitch them with compensation for the stolen artwork, which we can prove isn't legitimate, they'll play ball. We get to rob the museum, we get the artwork, they get compensation— and they can have a replacement piece purchased with the returned funds. Then, the escapade will be used as a part of a promotional campaign to boost the museum, your art, and bust the ring further."

"You still owe me all of the chicken wings I want tonight, Dean. Give me your reasons why her idea isn't sound."

"It might work. One of my brothers runs a security gig, and he has a good reputation. If he can't bust into their operations, they have tight security. It's not a bad idea. It's just riskier than I like."

"It's not risky if it's a security test, Dean."

"If Layla is at all involved, it's riskier than I like."

"Dean, you can't lock her in a bubble. Dad's talked to you about this before. You need to control your overprotective tendencies."

"My overprotective tendencies are the reason you're with me rather than still trotting around at Mom's heels with the other foals."

"That's not at all fair."

"But it's the truth."

"Fine. Layla can protect herself, and you're

just going to get used to it. Do the things she likes, which includes feeding her. She really likes when you feed her."

I did enjoy when he brought me food. As agreeing with Xena would ensure more incidents involving him feeding me, I nodded. "It's true. I do really like when I receive food."

"There. Pamper her that way. Treat her to new food every day. She can take care of herself in potentially dangerous situations. Also? After seeing her take down a man much bigger than her without batting an eye over it, I'm not at all concerned. Give her something blunt to carry around in her purse. Her quest to transform it into a shank might leave the bastard alive. If we give her a knife, she'll have to tell the judge why she killed someone during self-defense, and that'd stress you out."

"That'd stress me out?" Dean asked, and he pointed at me. "What about her?"

"Dean, does she look like she is at all bothered by having put a mere man back in his place after invading her space?"

As the pair would bicker if I let them, I said, "I'm not at all bothered. Honestly, I don't see what the big deal is. If the museum doesn't mind us trying to steal their stuff, it sounds like fun. I've never robbed a museum before. Honestly, I just took stuff because I didn't know how to pay for it. The card didn't make sense."

"The card still doesn't make much sense to you, but at least you understand how to use it," Xena muttered.

"I like the card even when I don't understand it. The card, so far, has purchased food. It would have bought art supplies if Dean hadn't used his card to do it. The card let me take these things and make them mine without me going to jail over it. Actually, I really like the card."

"See? Layla's easy to understand. She understands money goes onto the card, the card pays for the important things in life, like food and art supplies, and that she can earn money through painting to put onto the card. That's the bases covered. Now we just need to teach her the little details, like rent, landlords, mortgages, and taxes."

Dean ran a hand through his hair and scratched his scalp. "This is going to be more complicated than I thought."

"Just go with the heist idea, Dean. First, she gets one of her paintings back, and we can teach her how much she's actually worth. Of course, teaching her the value of money will be a challenge, but we'll get there eventually. As long as she doesn't try to buy a bunch of cars, expensive jewelry, or things like that, her card will work."

"Can I just ask you if it's okay to buy something? That seems easier."

Xena shook her head. "You do need to learn how to count, what money is worth, and so on. You need to stay independent, and Dean can't handle your money all the time."

"Like hell I can't."

"You're not allowed."

"I don't see why not."

"Layla needs to be self-reliant."

"No, she doesn't."

"Yes, she does. Also, you're a blight on this Earth!"

One unicorn was trouble. Two was double trouble. What kind of trouble would having an entire herd of them in the same place create? "Before you two settle in for a fight, can we order something to eat? I'm okay with you fighting as long as I can have something to eat. After I eat, I can paint while you two fight. I'll observe you while I paint. It'll be entertaining, I think. Watching you two fight is much more entertaining than a prison fight. I'm somewhat confident you're not going to shank each other. I draw a line there. The only one who can shank people is me. That's my job."

"We won't fight all night because Dean is going to call Mom and Dad. They're going to bring in the entire herd, and we're going to deal with this ring ourselves. Dean will justify this on his quest to secure a mare for himself. That's you, Layla. But yes, you can paint tonight, and we'll see about moving on to-morrow if your painting is okay to move. If not, we'll stay here for a few days and relax in the hotel room while you enjoy yourself painting. We're not on a timetable. Our mission is already completed. Dean wanted you, and you're here."

Dean would drive me crazier than I already was within a few days. "Can you ask when they're taking him in to have his head examined?"

Xena cackled. "I should, but no. Dean likes artsy women with at least half a brain. Sure, you're uneducated, but you're smart. You pick up concepts really quickly from what I've seen, and well, you're ridiculously nice."

"Xena," Dean warned.

"What? She deserves to know you're out for her. I mean, I've flat-out told her you want to take her to bed, and she hasn't run yet. I'm going to do you a big favor, Dean. I suggested you would buy all sorts of warm blankets you'd pile on your bed to lure her there, and she didn't seem against the idea. Don't worry so much. If she didn't want you around, she'd just knee you in the groin and take you out with the nearest blunt object she might be able to convert into a shiv."

"She's not wrong. My general reaction to people entering my space that I don't want there is violence. I'd also like to point out that this doesn't make me a very nice person."

"You shared your first cupcake with us. That permanently puts you into the ridiculously nice category. Also, you're excessively patient. I observed this from your activities in the clothing store and the art supply store. Anyway, he's not a bad choice, and I approve any taming of my brother you wish to do."

"I'm so glad I have your approval."

"You also have a masterful grasp of sarcasm."

I sat on the floor and began the tedious process of sorting through my painting supplies. I organized my paints by color, put the primers to the side and investigated my canvases, testing each one until I found one I thought would work well for my artistic interpretation of the troublesome stallion. "Can I listen to Dean's part of the conversation when he calls?"

"Would you like to hear the entire conversation?" Xena asked, tilting her head to the side. "You can if you want."

"That's possible? There's no intercom here."

"I like that you know how intercoms work but aren't aware that phones have a speaker function. Dean, you may as well text Dad and warn him you'll be calling and that they'll be on speaker. You may as well confess a convict has turned your head, and that you've lost all sense and plan on making her your mare the instant she agrees."

"Xena!"

"What? I'm establishing the situation so Layla knows what's going on. For some reason, I don't think she's going to understand if you flirt with her. I'd like you to survive your courtship."

It pained me she told the truth and nothing but the truth. "I do have a bad habit of hitting people who get in my space. She's probably right."

"I'm expecting challenges. I wouldn't want to become bored. I certainly hope you won't become bored, either."

Was Dean out of his mind? Boredom ruled in prison even more than the guards, and I supposed my love of painting had been found in my escape from the monotony of daily life. Day in, day out, I'd lived by a routine.

"Is it odd that I don't miss the routine?"

Dean's brow furrowed. "What do you mean?"

"Every day, it was the same. We woke every day near dawn. Sometimes before, depending on the time of year. We would have fifteen minutes to exercise. They would use the intercom to direct us. Then, we either went to work or waited. Those who didn't have work could make calls. A lot did. Sometimes, they'd talk about their conversations. A few contacted their attorneys. Others spoke to their families. They were rarely gone long. If a lot of people wanted to make calls, they'd rotate them through in shifts. I never bothered with calling any of my attorneys. They'd show up. I didn't really care when they showed up. Others did."

Dean sighed. "Well, that will change, not that I have any plans to allow anyone to take you back to prison. You'd be able to call me."

"You'd rather call me. I'm prettier."

She was? I looked her over, and then I turned my attention to Dean. Of the two, I definitely preferred him. "Will you survive if I disagree with you?"

"No."

"That's a shame. I actually like you. How would you like to be buried? Do unicorns prefer to be buried or burned?"

"We're not picky. We usually abide by our home culture." Xena wrinkled her nose. "In my case, I'd be buried with personal possessions after undergoing various rituals to make sure I remained dead or at least benevolent after death. Should I die, the herd will make a pilgrimage to the land of my birth with my remains. If it's far away, I will be burned on a pyre and my bones would be taken for interment. I suppose I might have to survive just this once, as the amount of effort my brother would have to invest in my burial would distress him."

"How generous of you."

"Dean, I resent your awful method of finding a mare. Really. What sort of stallion picks someone interesting from an active convict list and arranges for her parole?"

"A good one," Dean replied. "We'll get to have a herd bonding experience because of it, too."

"I do have to admit, taking over a counterfeit art ring will be a lot of fun. And the museum heist! We can't forget the museum heist. Please tell our parents about the heist."

"We'll be on speaker. You can tell them yourself. You're the one who wants to try to pull off a heist as part of a security test. I wish you the best of luck with that, by the way. You're going to have to convince the entire herd and Layla to play along with that nonsense."

"It will be worth it."

"I hope so, because you're going to have to handle all the real work. I will be busy teaching Layla."

"One of you is actually going to teach me something?" I grimaced. "Well, outside of how to use my card and buy things."

"I'm going to go over the receipt for all of your art supplies with you tomorrow, and we're going to practice writing. When you're not doing that, you'll paint. Xena will handle organizing the herd. We'll hole up here for at least another few days while we get everyone coordinated. It'll also make it harder for this ring to get a hold of you."

Life had gotten complicated, but for a change, I looked forward to what the future would bring.

EIGHT

There are other men in the world.

DEAN WASTED ALMOST an hour deciding if he would call his father, and his expression implied he expected to be attending his execution. Without any idea of what to expect, I focused on my painting. Until I got to test my new oil paints, I had no idea if it would take hours, days, or even months to fully dry. Some of the paints I'd used had taken weeks, resulting in me working on many paintings at the same time while I waited to be able to work on one again.

I wanted to paint Dean to perfection, and I couldn't afford to be hasty, not with oil paints.

Maybe I should've acquired acrylics so I could have more instant gratification.

Instead of the perfect canvas I'd selected, I grabbed one of the panels and went to work. On the panel, I'd experiment and perfect his form, and then I'd do my best work on the canvas. If the panel didn't dry well enough to move, I wouldn't regret its loss, either.

"Are you going to call?" Xena sat nearby and watched me work. "I thought you were going to work on canvas, Layla."

"I don't know how long it takes this paint to dry, so I'll use a test panel. If it gets ruined because we have to go somewhere else before it dries, then it's okay. And I'll know what to expect from the paint."

"We can find a way to preserve the painting even if we have to move it wet, even if I have to find someone to hire to protect it."

"It's better to see how it dries naturally."

Xena chuckled. "Have it your way, then. Dean, will you just call already? I don't know why you're being a wuss over this."

"What if they don't like Layla?"

"In good news, neither Mom nor Dad have to worry about marrying Layla. It's not their problem. The herd isn't marrying her. You would be, assuming you can convince her. Also, Layla? Just because Dean came around first doesn't mean you have to accept him. There are other men in the world."

"I'm aware. I've met a lot of them in prison. I've kneed more than I can readily count in the groin for getting into my space. So far, Dean hasn't gotten into my space in an unacceptable fashion, which puts him far above the usual fare."

Dean grimaced. "I feel like I should say that there are a lot of good men in the world. They just don't tend to be found in prison."

"I'd certainly hope not." Shaking my head, I browsed my selection of pale colors so I could attempt to capture Dean at his best. Or his worst.

Painting such a naughty unicorn to be majestic would test my skills.

"But seriously, Layla. Only go with my brother's insanity if you actually like him, think you'll get along with him for a damned long time, and you want to stay with him. You don't have to decide right away. You can date him for a decade or two before you decide if you want. Conversion will reset your biological clock."

"My what?"

"Your body's age, ability to have children, and general health. Basically, after conversion, you won't be a human anymore. You'll be stuck with Dean, but as I said, there are far worse stallions you could be stuck with."

"Stuck?" Dean complained.

"I just said there were far worse stallions she could be stuck with. I'm making sure she's able to make an educated decision, as she's been barred from doing that her entire life. I won't have your starry eyes railroading her. My first act as world ruler is to make sure she is the one who makes the final choice. I figured you were hopeless from the instant you read about her while doing your best to save the world rather than take it over."

"Is that how unicorns are? There are those who want to save the world, like Dean, and then there are those who want to take over the world, like you. Are there other types?"

"The ones that want to stab everything, the ones that like to light things on fire so they can eat the ashes, and the ones that would prefer to drown their victims, stab them, and drain them of their blood post drowning. We don't talk about those ones all that much. That's one thing the other unicorn species have in common: we don't like the kelpie imposters."

"Kelpie imposters?"

"Kelpies are water demons. They lack horns, often lure people into water to either drown them or breed with them and take the shape of horses. Those so-called 'unicorns' act like kelpies, but they're blood drinkers. They're related to Eastern unicorns, except they're a lot nastier. There are several species of Eastern unicorns, and some of them do drink blood and eat meat, but they prefer scavenging battlefields. Our species gets along well with most, but we also don't get involved in the species feuds. And let me tell you, some of the other species of unicorns?

They'll fight to the death if they run into each other. And if we happen to be around when a fight like that happens, we're expected to wade in, kick them both into submission, drive them off, and tell them to leave each other alone. We're usually considered the 'nice' unicorns. We are so not nice, not when we're peacekeeping. Really, we can be nasty if pushed."

"Is that why you don't view my tendency to shank people as a bad thing?"

"Well, we won't have to teach you how to wade in and knock heads together. That's a point to Dean. Dean, just call already."

"Fine, fine. I'm calling." Dean tapped the screen of his phone and set it on the coffee table. "This is a terrible idea."

The phone rang and I dabbed white, black, a selection of warm and cool grays, and brown paint onto my palette. As always when starting a painting featuring a person or animal, I began with his head and eyes.

The eyes were windows to the soul, and if I couldn't paint his eyes well, the rest of the painting would fall apart. It would take effort to capture so much stubborn pride, ego, and mischief, but the challenge thrilled me.

Dean's brown eyes wouldn't impress most, but I liked the color, a rich tone full of life.

"There's something seriously wrong with

you, boy, to take an hour to actually call after texting," a man announced. "I ought to come over there and teach you a thing or two about manners."

In prison language, a threat like that would result in a fight, and I debated if Dean required assistance or if he should face his father's wrath on his own. I figured the stallion could handle himself, and I went to work capturing him in paints. The brown I'd chosen lacked the depth I wanted, and I grabbed every brown I could in search of the right one. Then, as I doubted just brown would work, I grabbed a few yellows, oranges, and reds to add some fire to the color.

"Sorry, Dad. There's a situation and Xena convinced me to ask the herd for a favor."

"You have my attention. For you to let your sister talk you into anything, the world must surely be ending. Is there a reason we're talking in English?"

"Layla speaks English, and she's listening. It'd be rude to switch to a different language when we're going to be talking about her."

"Who is Layla?"

Xena snickered. "She's the convict he plucked out of court and is determined to convert into a pretty little mare for himself. He's positively smitten. She's tolerant, although she's definitely listening to his overtures, which have involved teaching her how life outside of prison works. She's been incarcerated since she was five or six."

"Okay. While I'm well versed on the existence of demonic little children, of which you are only one of many, I would not say any little filly that age deserves incarceration in an actual prison. The corner typically works along with other parental methods. Explain."

"Her mother hated her and wanted to get rid of her. So, she did. It turns out Layla's a talented painter, and there's a counterfeit art ring taking advantage of her abilities. She had no way of knowing she was participating in illegal activities, and she's quite possibly the sweetest human I've had the pleasure of meeting. I like her, but I want to make sure she understands how life is supposed to work before she tames Dean. I don't see him taming her. You also won't have to train her much on the self-defense front. She tried to shank someone with my purse."

Dean and Xena's father whistled. "I need to remember when I ask you, my daughter, for an explanation, it's going to be far worse than I imagined possible. From the day you were born, you were trouble, Xena."

"Hey! It's not my fault this time. Dean was whining he wanted a mare he could pamper, and he was tired of human women who wanted to bang him for his money. So, he got bored and decided to take advantage of our rarity rating to troll the prison system for someone interesting. He found her, and he couldn't understand how someone with a string of petty thefts was serving a life sentence in a high security prison."

"The more you talk, Xena, the more worried I become. Dean? What do you have to say for yourself?"

"She slapped my ass in court and fed me part of her first cupcake. How could I say no to that?"

I grinned at the awkward silence. It would be difficult to paint him as anything other than naughty. Did I even want to? I could paint him as majestic while naughty. That would be a challenge.

"Xena?"

"She really did. She was on her way to the witness stand and gave him a slap right to his rump. He about jumped out of his skin, and she got lucky he didn't clip her with a hoof. He would've suffered a meltdown if he had, too. I thought I'd have to sit on him during the court session. Her statements upset him. There's probably records of the session somewhere. They brought in an angel because of the circumstances, and Layla inadvertently exposed the counterfeit ring. I think the angel became upset over the reality of Layla's life and purchased her the type of cupcake she'd stolen. Turns out nobody had taught her how to use her debit card. That card? Has tens of thousands of available dollars on it. We have the information for it, and the court is handling restitutions for her, but her current confirmed owed earnings are already on it. Dean won't let her use her card while he's around, though. She's painting right now, which is all she really knows. I took her to the art store while Dean was getting his US license and buying a vehicle. We bought too much. Also, when you bring the herd, please get a big SUV. We're going to need it to move her new clothes and her art supplies. Can you ask Simon if he can preserve wet oil paintings? We might have to move her in-progress art before it has a chance to dry."

"I'm sure Simon can manage. Why am I gathering the herd and invading the United States?"

"Well, two members of the counterfeit ring have attempted to kidnap her once already. She kneed the one in the groin and did her best to shank him with my purse. They ran away—the cowards. I was debating how best to beat them, but she took care of it herself."

"That's a fair reason for concern. Dean, what are your thoughts on this, son?"

"They're damned lucky I was at the courthouse snarling at a judge when it happened, as I would have left bloody smears on the road for even thinking about trying to touch her."

"And what is the young lady's opinion on all of this?"

Both Xena and Dean stared at me. I continued to paint the naughty unicorn's eyes, hoping I could capture just how much trouble he'd inevitably create wherever he went. In fact, the more exposure to the pair I had, the more I believed they were wolves in sheep's clothing. "Neither should be left unsupervised. I'm not sure a maximum-security prison cell could hold either for long and we still haven't ordered chicken wings yet. Or baked treats."

"I'll make sure you're fed after we're done talking to Dad," Dean promised. "And we'd have to move your painting station so we can get to the door."

I considered my placement near the door, art supplies spread out in a sea around me. "That's a valid point. I accept responsibility for the delay. But you owe me extra chicken wings still."

"I'll get you some cheese sticks to try to go with them, and I'll see if there are any bakeries that'll deliver. If not, there's a convenience store down the street. They won't have great stuff, but they'll have some stuff. Either way, you'll have some form of baked good to go with dinner tonight."

"It's rare for a woman to make things like dinner selection easy, Dean. Appreciate this while it lasts," his father advised. "Your mother goes out of her way to make me guess. She likes when I put in the extra effort. She also likes when I take the foals with me so she can indulge in peace and quiet."

"Mom isn't there, is she?"

"She is indulging in some peace and quiet right now. I was told if the foals woke her, she would geld me. As I'm not sure if she's serious this time, the foals and I made a tent fort. As building a tent fort is tiring work, I'm the only conscious person in the house, as it's one in the morning."

Dean grimaced. "Right. It's late there. Sorry, Dad."

"If you'd called me over something frivolous, I might've cared, but it seems you two have gotten yourselves in trouble. Again. You're going to have to give me an idea of what you want us to do so we can prepare before I bring the herd over. Obviously, preventing them from kidnapping your mare is at the top of the list. You wouldn't call in the entire herd for just that. Well, you might, but Xena wouldn't. She's sensible sometimes. I'm expecting you to forgo any sensibility for the next ten or so years, just like your brothers and sisters. Your choice of hunting grounds is a little unusual, but I suppose desperate times lead to desperate measures. Try not to upset your mare too much before you convince her she should stick around."

Xena laughed. "She's painting Dean as a unicorn right now. She made him model for her for hours, and he danced to her tune without a peep of complaint. I'm scheduled for a turn, but she took pity on me on account of this phone call and dinner. So far, I think she's painting his head. Hey, Layla?"

"Hmm?"

"Is it normal for it to take such a long time to paint so very little?"

"I'm experimenting, so yes. I like experimenting."

In reality, I wasn't sure which method of painting would best portray the troublesome stallion, so I'd have to play around with it until I found the way I liked best.

"I think we've lost her to her painting, Dad. I tried."

"You didn't try very hard, but if she's happy using painting as a coping mechanism, then I say that's more Dean's problem than mine right now. Back on subject. What do you need us for?"

"Well, since the counterfeiting ring isn't going to stop until they either get Layla back or make sure no one else has her, I thought we'd get together, wipe the ring out, expose all the paintings they forged using her, and offer to buy the paintings back so Layla can have them. We can then sell them after the story is exposed and we figure out how they authenticated the paintings. I figure at least one of her paintings has to be in a museum, so we should test their security. We would tell them we're doing it, and if we can't bust in, their art should be safe. If we bust in, they sell the painting to us after we steal it."

"You just want to steal things again," their father accused.

"Well, yes. And Layla's always stolen things she shouldn't, not that that's really her fault. But it's not stealing if we're allowed to go in and test their security. I get to steal something, and it's legal. Best of all, if we con the museum into trying to buy another piece of art from the counterfeiters, we could run our heist the same time the museum folks are negotiating for the new painting!"

"No."

"Dad," Xena whined. "It's a brilliant idea."

"I could get the contact information for the painting sellers and accomplish the same thing. I'm not against having Simon or Juan test their security work against a museum, but we're not turning it into more of a mad-house than such a venture would be. And while I'll bring the herd over, we'll need to do some serious discussion and research into the situation. Here's what you're going to do. You're going to lay low, and you'll help Dean's young lady settle. If she's been in prison for a long time, she will have difficulties adjusting."

"She's been okay so far," Xena replied. "She's really resilient."

"Well, she'll have to be to put up with Dean."

The stallion sighed. "That's not at all fair, Dad."

"It really is. Don't get into any trouble while I'm gone. Also, I suggest you acclimate Layla to hugging and physical contact. You know your mother." The line clicked.

Dean picked up his phone, glaring at the screen. "He really hung up on me."

"Well, it is late there, and if Mom made him build a pillow fort, Mom or one of the foals isn't feeling well, so he's going to have to deal with someone sick on a long flight. He probably wants to call Juan and get him on the move here. Don't be surprised if he shows up tomorrow morning."

"Juan?" While puzzled by the entire phone conversation and their father's parting warning, I would find out what he'd meant soon enough.

"My older brother. He enjoys security work, and he's our oldest brother's right-hand man. Juan is the doer; Simon is the thinker. I bet Dad's on the phone with Juan now, as he loves bodyguard roles, and the instant he learns I'm interested in you, he'll be over here putting me in my place and making sure I treat you right while showing me how I ought to protect you."

I could think of exactly one way to deal with the problem. "If he tries that with me, I'm breaking his nose on your thick skull."

Xena's eyes widened, and Dean scowled. I returned to my painting, making a mental note I'd have to study him when angry so I could capture his fury in oil.

He'd be spectacular, a living contradiction on the canvas. I resumed my work, determined to capture his every emotion and immortalize it.

"I think she means it, Dean."

"Oh, I know she means it. I'm just debating if it's worth getting a concussion for the pleasure of watching her break his face with my hard head. You know what? It is. Should you have any urges to break my brother's nose on my head, I'll cooperate. Just try not to kill either one of us. You'd make Xena cry."

"I might cry, for all of five seconds. Then I'd start going over my share of the inheritance."

"You would miss me. Admit it, Xena. You'd miss that your only older brother willing to let you tag along was gone. You'd have to move back in with Mom and Dad for at least five years."

"You're right. I would miss you. I would also miss freedom. You can't kill him beating up Juan, Layla."

"I can't make him pose for me if he's dead. I'll spare him for however long he remains an interesting painting subject."

Dean sighed. "You know what? I'll take it. If posing for your artistic enjoyment makes you happy, I shall endeavor to be an interesting painting subject for you."

"How many unicorns am I going to have to beat up?" If I had to make plans to tenderize a lot of unicorns, I'd need to do my stretches, or I'd pull a muscle.

Xena grimaced. "Hopefully, just Juan. That said, we're going to have to test how well you can handle hugs and displays of affection. Mom's a hugger, and the instant Dad tells her about you, she will be weepy and want to hug you until she's absolutely certain you know you're loved. Mom's hardly delicate, but Dad'll freak if you get into a brawl with Mom. I am curious which one of you would win, but not curious enough to risk Dad's wrath over it. I think Mom would win. She's got a lot of experience correcting Dad when he steps out of line and wrangling stubborn colts. And sometimes, once Dad gets into a mood, she has one of two ways of dealing with him."

"Dare I ask?"

"You do."

I laughed at her immediate reply. "Okay. How does she deal with him?"

"She either flattens him or takes him to bed. And let me tell you, there are more than a few foals in this family because Mom tamed Dad taking him to bed."

Some things I didn't need to know, and that went onto the list in a fairly high position. "I'm not responsible for any new brothers or sisters you might have in the future."

"I'm sure Mom's already got a foal on the way. She's been gunning after Dad for months. If she's not, we're going to have to spend at least an hour taunting Dad, after which we'll surely be graced with a new brother or sister." Xena rubbed her hands together. "The next one means they might forget about me for a whole decade!"

"Keep dreaming, Xena," Dean muttered.

"Have a foal or two. They'll forget about me for sure, then."

"Neither of our parents are going to forget about you, so give it up. If they haven't forgotten about Juan, and you know full well they haven't, there is no chance they're going to forget about you. If you don't want them nosing about in your love life, just tell them you're looking around but haven't found the right stud quite yet. Take pictures of men you find appealing, but make sure you record things Mom won't like about them. Then, tell them you were looking at one, but it wouldn't work out and why. You'll get at least six months of mileage per man that way."

"Wow. There's a method to your madness, Dean?"

"You've been following me around for years and you're just figuring this out?"

I sensed another argument on the horizon, which amused me more than anything else. "Before you settle in to fight, can you order dinner, please? If you two start bickering before food is ordered, we'll all starve."

"I'll help her make a path to the door; you order food. Tomorrow is going to be a long day."

Of that, I had no doubt.

NINE

I will break your face on Dean's
head.

I MEANT to resume painting after dinner, but
I ate too much, which proved my undoing.
Dean, in an effort to acclimate me to people
touching me, had insisted I stretch out on the
couch with my feet on his lap. As the unicorns expected I'd react with violence to
them coming into my space without accli-
mating me to it, Dean started exposing me to
affection through a foot rub.

As far as I was concerned, his hands and
my feet could begin a long-term relationship.
I found his attention so relaxing I dozed off.

A knock at the door woke me, and Dean
patted my leg. "Relax, Layla. That's just Juan.
He caught the first flight out of Mexico. He
called me. You slept through it."

Xena bounced to the door, opened it, and
a Hispanic man strolled in, a few streaks of
gray in his dark hair. With a smile, he kissed

Xena's cheek. "Where's this little mare Dad says I have to keep an eye on else we all suffer Dean's wrath?"

I stretched, rolled off the couch, and got to my feet, keeping an eye on Juan while I went through the motions of preparing for the day. "While I'm little, I'm not a mare."

"Yet," Juan announced, strolling over.

Dean stood, and the instant the Hispanic man came into my reach, I dove for Juan, slammed one fist into his gut, and slapped my hand against the back of his head. I debated between Dean's head or the coffee table as my target but opted against both. Instead, I patted him as a warning of what I could have done before letting him go. "If I can grab you, you're in my space. If your name isn't Dean, and you enter my space, I will break your face on Dean's head."

"Well," Juan wheezed out, "I see Dad wasn't joking when he'd warned me you liked your women feisty."

"I wouldn't call her feisty. I'd call her proactive in self-defense. That, plus I told her she could break your nose on my head whenever she wanted."

"I don't know what I did to upset you, but I apologize. Good form, lady. And if I offended you calling you a mare, I'm sorry. However, can I ask why you'd use Dean's head to break my face? What did my face and his head do?"

"His head is the hardest surface in this hotel room."

"But what about my face?"

I pointed at Dean. "Blame him."

"Dean, what did you tell her?"

"I didn't, not really. I was trying to tell her about the family. It went poorly."

"I can't imagine why." Juan straightened his shoulders and grimaced. "Your lady hits hard. Dad said you plucked her out of prison?"

"I nudged North Carolina about her when I saw the court entry for a cupcake theft. She interested me." Dean's tone implied his interest covered more than base curiosity. "I looked into her public records, and well, she's got a history."

"I'm not sure Mom or Dad are going to be happy you were looking for a wife in the prison system."

"If I wanted a wilting lily, I would've gone with one of the women our mother suggested."

"Mom does keep throwing delicate ladies at you, this is true. I'm not sure what she's thinking, really. You're not the kind to be happy if you can step on your partner. You want her to have fight." Juan grimaced and glanced at me. "Maybe you went to an extreme."

"I probably should have discouraged her from wanting to break your nose, but you're an ass, so I figured you deserved whatever she did to you. You're supposed to be a strong man working security. You should be able to protect yourself from Layla. I'm grateful she didn't introduce your nose to my skull, though."

"I thought about it, but then I figured it would take a long time to get the blood out of your hair. I've already heard what your blood can do to an unsuspecting woman, so I think I'll stop just before making him bleed."

Dean laughed. "You wouldn't be unsuspecting. Conversion is a lengthy process. You'd be well aware of the entire process. And I wouldn't make you pretend you're a vampire for a few years."

After taking a few moments to think about it, I headed for the bathroom. The first night out of prison hadn't bothered me too much, but I missed the rigid structure of my morning. "Don't kill your brother without me, Dean."

"I can work around that."

A shower would do me a world of good. It took me a few minutes to figure out, but I got the water spraying at a comfortable temperature and went through my routine the same way I had done countless days before a pair of unicorns had turned my predictable life upside down. I questioned Dean's motives, his willingness to gamble on an unknown with a record, and everything that had happened in the past few whirlwind days.

Worse, I questioned my willingness to consider his strange ploy to add me to his world. Permanently. I intended to take my time washing my hair, but the longer I took, the more anxious I became, expecting a cranky guard to cut the water to the shower. They'd never barged into my cell, but the threat of doing that haunted my memories.

I emerged from the bathroom unnerved by the lack of everything I expected from my life. Dean and Juan sat on the couch and chatted while Xena struggled to make sense of my painting supplies. She stared at the spray can of fixer meant to preserve a sketch, something I hadn't used yet on my picture of Dean.

It sank in that the rest of my life would become a mystery, one I'd have to live each and every day, the unknown stretching before me. In prison, I'd feared things, but I knew what would come. The brief times I'd been free, I'd never expected to stay free long.

Freedom had been an unobtainable dream, and I'd never thought much about what I would do once I walked under the sun unchained.

"Everything okay, Layla?" Dean asked.

"What happens next?" I asked, afraid of confessing my growing doubt over how the rest of my life would play out.

My broken routine dumped me into a reality I had no idea how to handle.

No matter how they tried to reassure me, I couldn't paint myself a future.

The unicorns exchanged glances. While Dean and Xena floundered, Juan rose to his feet, circled the coffee table, and stepped right out of my reach. "What do you want to happen next?"

Something about his stance reminded me of the hardest men the prison had to offer, a living promise of violence brewing on a stormy horizon. I tensed. "I don't know."

"Well, that's a problem. You've been conditioned to a strict schedule, and you're now in a chaotic environment where you're encouraged and expected to set your own schedule. You're not the first ex-convict I've worked with. You see me, and I'm a threat because you know that people who stand like me are inclined towards violence. That's what my body language is telling you, and you don't know how to process the mixed signals. Logically, you know I'm here to help, and that I'm their brother. But my body language is sending you the only message you know to trust. Dean's body language is typically relaxed. He comes across as harmless, doesn't he? He's not, but he is much better at putting on an act than I am."

"Why do you work with ex-convicts?"

"I give them purpose after prison. Jails in Mexico are pretty rough. From what I've read, it's been pretty rough for you. There was a notation in your record of more than fifty incidents of violence flagged as self-defense. You're not that old. But you don't know how old you are, do you?"

"It's a number."

"The number is going to get a lot weirder. Dean, how old did the records you look at claim she is?"

"Twenty-seven."

"She's sixty-seven."

Dean's mouth dropped open, and he pointed at me. "There is no way she is sixty-seven, Juan. She looks in her twenties. She looks a little young for twenty-seven, but I figured that was because she was kept healthy by the guards so they wouldn't lose their painter."

"Yeah. I hacked the system last night while waiting for my morning flight. I wanted to get a good idea of what we were working with. Every ten years, they'd lose her in the system, move her to a different prison, and start her over. They were getting ready to move her again and lose her in the system again. I got the names of the guards who were consistent through her file, and I hacked their systems to find out more about them and their efforts. I suspect they have been working with a demon of some sort to alter her memories somewhat each time they've moved her."

"But Dad sends me a card every year on my birthday."

"Your mother disappeared shortly after your birth, and your father has been dead for a very long time. I'm sorry. I don't know who left you in a prison to rot. I wasn't able to find that information out in the short time I was able to research your case. Nothing you know is real, and I realize that's going to be hard for you to accept. I'd rather tell you the truth now than have you discover it for yourself later."

I frowned. "How old is sixty-seven?"

"The average lifespan of a human woman is seventy-four without significant medical or magical intervention. She's older than you are, Dean."

"But she seems so young," Xena whispered.

"I figure her species has something to do with that. She's probably just reaching maturity as her species. I'm not even sure you'll be able to convert her depending on what she actually is. She's not a demon or devil; there's no way one would emerge out of prison so infernally sweet. And that's one thing that was documented in the files I found. They can't break her. They've tried."

Dean's expression changed, and something dark burned in his eyes. "Who?"

"If I told you, there would be a lot of murders at your hand, and I don't feel like cleaning up that many bodies this week. She doesn't need a mass murderer. We don't have enough information to act. So, you have some decisions to make. You have sixty or so years of conditioning to undo. She's been spending every day adhering to a very specific routine. I have a copy of her usual schedule. You're going to have to put her in a structured environment until she breaks out of that herself. She's used to obeying, and there'll be problems if you toss her into a new life where she has to decide everything."

"She was happiest in the art supply store," Xena announced.

"That's what she knows. That's a common issue with long-term prisoners. Outside of prison, they gravitate towards what they know. That's why I get so many ex-convicts. They understand security. They understand the system. They understand the work, and they know how to make that fit the life they know. I've had a few life convictions get out early, and the first thing they do is shower and exercise in the morning. Give her twenty minutes, and she'll be itching to get in her exercise. If you tell her you're rescheduling it for later in the day and establish a new schedule, it'll be okay, but habit is hard to break and she's been in that habit longer than you've been alive."

"I can't be that old." Saying it didn't help. Too many doubts crept in. "And what do you mean about my species?"

"There is no way you're a human." Juan pulled out a phone and showed me a picture of an older woman. "This is what a woman closer to your real age looks like. Like Dean said, you look like you're in your late twenties —a little younger, really. But there are plenty of long-lived species. Look at Xena and Dean. They're closer to middle aged in human years, but they're both very young in unicorn standards. Some lines of unicorns are shorter lived than others. But our line? We live a long time. Our ancestors lived before the flood."

"The flood? What flood?"

"Noah's flood. He changed the face of the Earth in a catastrophe. Nobody really knows why, but it's compared to a preliminary End of Days."

"What's that?"

"The end of the world and life as we know

it as prophesied according to the Christian faith. Honestly, a lot of faiths have such things, and it's the one thing that is consistent. All faiths will converge at the End of Days. In that one case, they'll all be right. It will be a time of chaos and destruction, but once it's over, the Earth will be reborn, and the cycle will begin again. Light and dark, good and evil, all things in opposition will exist before life is renewed. We're just here to make the most of the time we do have. That's one of the things that long-lived races have. We may very well get to see the end of all things. Honestly, I prefer the way my people handled things."

"Your people?"

"A tribe in Mexico. I'll spare you from trying to pronounce it. We'd lose several hours. Or, possibly not. It depends. Some species, like us, can understand any language." Juan's eyes narrowed. "Art transcends language, so it's possible it doesn't matter what language I speak."

"May as well try it. It's not like this will get more complicated, and it would explain her grasp of English."

Juan said something in another language, one I'd never heard before, almost lyrical in its intonations while still possessing a hard, wild edge. "Did you understand that?"

I shook my head.

Dean scowled. "She may not have, but I did."

Juan smirked. "I know."

"What did you say?"

"You'd make a beautiful sacrifice on a bloody altar to save the world from the wrath of our hungering gods. Your heart's blood has the worth of a hundred or more men without question."

"That's oddly sweet yet horribly barbaric."

"My people believed sacrificing people would stave off the end of the world. It was a great honor to be chosen for sacrifice if you were willing, and those guilty of great crimes were sacrificed so their deaths would have value."

"Do you think it worked?" I asked, tilting my head to the side.

"Who knows? We're still here, so perhaps. I was born shortly before the conquistadors came and wiped my people out. I'm the last. It was in a time where Mom and Dad had us foals mingle with those of our homelands. Xena was the first foal who was taken from her homeland before she learned their ways. But they faced genocide, and they weren't going to risk her life. Dad has made several forays back to learn what he can of her culture, but they're all but gone, too. That's why Mom and Dad are in Europe right now. They can have a foal or two in a culture that is less likely to be wiped out. They're tired of watching our people die. But we're also all that's left."

Xena sighed and shrugged. "They try, and that's what matters, right? We're living legacies, Layla. Mom and Dad have lived among countless cultures. They remember long after humans forget. They remember the true history, not the one the winners present to the world to see. They've watched civilizations rise and fall. But that's what we are. We're history and myth on the hoof."

"So much for the idea that you're creatures of purity and innocence."

"Anything but. That's just another myth. Now, we're among the nicer species of unicorns, but we'll still kill and eat you if you really piss us off. We're just slower to anger than some of our brethren."

My brows shot up. "You eat people?"

"Humans are best grilled, but I'll take one or two raw every now and then."

I couldn't tell if he was joking, and I turned to Dean. "Is he serious?"

"He hasn't eaten anyone for a few hundred years. I'm currently participating in a human-free diet, nor have I been on any battle-grounds. During times of war, vultures weren't the only ones to clear a battlefield. Unicorns often helped. Some species more than other, but yeah. He's serious. Leaving human bodies around to rot is rude, so we help get rid of them. We do like helping to prevent the spread of disease."

As I couldn't tell if he was joking, too, I turned to Xena.

"It's true. Don't looked so shocked. Our kind was around long before humans even learned they could tame fire or speak. We try not to eat people now, but I figure we're a better choice than others. I mean, there are demonic corpse eaters. Which would you rather have take care of your body? It's a lot faster for us to take care of the bodies, too."

"But how?"

Xena smiled. "Magic, of course. We don't particularly like the taste of human, really. But it's part of what we are. We're drawn to battlegrounds that haven't been put to peace. We send the spirits of the departed on their way. We take flesh as our price of shepherding. Usually we take a nibble or two from each body before shepherding, and then we strip the remaining decaying flesh from their corpses and destroy it to prevent the spread of disease. Eating a bite lets us do all that work. But we can't destroy the decaying flesh without that bite."

I couldn't decide if unicorns were fantastic or fantastically awful. "How long does it take for you to dispose of a body that way?"

"About three seconds a corpse. Our herd

can graze down an entire battlefield in an afternoon," Xena announced with pride in her voice. "We all learn how to do it, but Mom and Dad usually make us learn on deer or cattle. We get together and practice every few years. It's usually expensive unless there's a state doing a deer cull. They call us. Deer do not like us. They know we might hunt them. Our pretty horns are excellent weapons, and there's nothing more satisfying than hitting dinner at a full charge. We're taught to go for the kill in one hit. It's rude to draw out a death."

"You don't actively hunt humans?"

"Not usually. And don't listen to Dean. He's just upset over your circumstances. If they cross paths, I expect he'll charge and have a snack or ten. Or twenty. Juan? How many are in this ring?"

"I don't know. I hadn't gotten that far into my research. I'll need a few days to get a full list of participants."

It amazed me Juan had gotten so much information as it was in such a short period of time. "How did you learn all this in the first place?"

"The security business is really a business of knowledge. It's much easier to protect someone when I know what I have to protect them from. You're going to be a challenge. And no, Dean. You can't eliminate them yet."

"Yet," Dean echoed. "Clarify the yet."

"If someone threatens her while you're around, I won't tell Mom and Dad until after the trial. And I'll ask Clarence to handle your trial."

"Clarence?"

"An angel. He owes me a favor, and he'll have no problem informing the court Dean ate a human in defense of another. Particularly, in defense of the mare he wishes to breed with. They take that seriously. For some reason, unicorns are prized exotics they wish to preserve, and we're not exactly rabbits on the breeding department. Someone thought it was a good idea to give unicorns heightened rights to preserve our species. I mean, it's only a few meals, right?"

"That is disgusting. Please don't eat any humans you kill on my behalf, Dean."

"But I really should clean up after myself, Layla."

"No. You may stomp on the body, but you may not eat the body. Make someone else pay for the funeral. And does his soul really deserve to be guided to the afterlife?"

"Yes. Straight to the nastiest hell I can find. We can nudge souls in the direction we want them to go. I would not be a kind shepherd."

At a complete loss of what to say or think, I stared at him, my mouth hanging open.

"She's definitely not a demon or a devil. She'd be delighting in that if she were." Juan circled me, looking me over. "She's not a muse. She would've understood me if she was a muse. She's not an angel, either. At least not of the Christian faith or the similar faiths. I don't know what you are, but I want to find out, damn it. I hate not knowing something."

"Muse?" I asked. "What's that?"

Juan pointed at my art supplies. "Muses are Greek divines with an affiliation for the arts. There are nine of them at any given time, and a new one shows up when one dies. Muses can learn any language because art goes beyond all boundaries, and language is arguably an art. Muses can be a security problem, as they'll want to steal from museums to own art they fall in love with. They'll fixate on some art and refuse to stop until they possess it or get their fill. I've had to tango with a muse before. Honestly, I'm a little disappointed. Watching Dean try to handle a muse would've been interesting. Whatever you are, I'm sure it'll be fine. Unicorns can bond even to divines, although it's rare. And since conversion doesn't remove what you were before you become a unicorn, you can be converted and still be what you are now. It's a good deal for you. Except the eating people part, but Mom and Dad will teach you on deer. You might need the skill one day. And on a battlefield, you'll see why our job is important. Otherwise, there'd be a lot of ghosts in the world. We help them cross if they lose their way during a battle. That's common."

"You're sure I won't have to eat people if I agree to be converted?"

With a faint smile, Juan shook his head. "In modern times, we only do it if we're shepherding lost souls, and it's not what you think. You'll understand after your conversion. You'll be able to see the lost. They want to go, and we want them to go. It takes flesh and blood for us to send them on their way, but we can do it with their bones or ash, too. It's just harder. I'm from a rather bloodthirsty culture, so I'm far more enthusiastic about our duty than the rest of the family. Well, Mom gets pretty vicious sometimes, but while she'll lead the charge to the battlefield and even join in the fray, she's otherwise pacifistic. She's a lover until she gets onto a battlefield. Honestly, she's terrifying, but please don't tell her I said that."

"If I'm not human, what am I?"

"It's hard losing your sense of identity," Juan said, and his expression softened. "I don't have an answer for you. All I know is there's no way you're a human. But you're something—and you're probably something special. Someone went to a lot of trouble to hide you in North Carolina's legal system for sixty years, and they used every level of the judicial system to do it. You might even be older. They had a note that you appeared a certain age when you were entered into the system, but I wasn't able to find anything concrete. While the records I found listed your parents, you don't have a birth certificate. It's entirely possible the people listed as your parents aren't even your parents. Their deaths would just legalize you entering the system, but until we find proof of who you actually are, anything is possible."

"But I remember my mother."

"That woman wasn't your mother. As far as I know, she could've been a cradle robber, but she wasn't your mother; that much was confirmed in the files I found. Where you came from is a mystery. I'll do my best to solve it. Since you seem to be a long-lived species, it's entirely possible you were stolen, and your parents are still alive. Dean will not be happy to fight your real parents for you, but I'll find it entertaining. It's possible you're the child of a divine or two. It's not uncommon for children of the divine to have many of the traits of their parents. A muse for a mother might be an option. But muses don't tend to be quite so disgustingly pure."

"Could she be the child of a very odd triad?" Dean asked. "That would make some sense. Her kleptomaniac tendencies could be a contribution of her demonic ancestry, her general temperament from her angelic ancestry, and her artistic ability from her muse mother. Usually angels fall in with humans, but it's possible, isn't it?"

Juan frowned and considered me with deep lines creasing his forehead. "There was no DNA record. We could get a meter brought in and I could ask Clarence to confirm her heritage. The triad theory is interesting, but I'm not sure how plausible it'd be. The pantheons tend to get upset when their divines mingle. It confuses things. It's bad enough when their children mingle. I doubt she's the direct child of a triad, but if you had a muse who took a human man, and the child of a triad, and they had a child, someone like Layla might be born. There are a lot of cases where weird mixes are showing up and coming into their power. But she's been hidden in the system a long time. She would have to be one of the first grandchildren of a divine to be born this emergence. But that would make her age about right."

"Do you want to know, Layla?"

Already tired of not knowing who I was or why I'd been incarcerated for even longer than I thought, I nodded. "I do."

"Then I'll call in that favor. I expect it won't be long. Hold in there for a while,

Layla. You'll have answers sooner than later, especially if you have angelic blood. With rare exception, angels are sensitive about this sort of thing, even when they have to watch from a distance because *He* won't let them interfere in the workings of the mortal world. If we invite the hosts of heaven to us, they may meddle or they may not; it depends on *Him*."

All I could do was what I always did, which involved waiting for answers I might never get. "That doesn't sound promising."

Dean shook his head. "Angels hate injustice. One already got you a cupcake because she recognized the injustice of your situation. But nobody asked her what you are. The worst we'll learn is that Clarence doesn't know, and the DNA test isn't conclusive."

"And if he knows or the test is conclusive?"

"We'll deal with whatever happens when it happens," Dean promised. "Your heritage doesn't define you. You're you, and what you learn today won't change anything."

I wanted to believe him, but my doubts silenced my voice. I nodded, and I hoped my acceptance of his claim didn't become a lie.

TEN

I've been waiting a long time for this
moment.

JUAN MADE a phone call and said, "Clarence,
I'd like to call in that favor you owe me."

A moment later, an angel popped into the
room in a flash of golden light. "I've been
waiting a long time for this moment."

Despite having witnessed angels pop in
and out of existence before, I had to stop myself from grabbing the nearest blunt object
and making good use of it. I shook from the
effort of containing my initial instinct to remove the threat.

"We need to know what Layla is, who her
family is, and if she was stolen. I want to call
in my favor to learn everything we can about
her. I did research on her through the prison
system; everything I found indicates she's
been a victim for a long time."

The angel strode towards to me and I
tensed.

"It is not like you to use something as valuable as a boon from an angel purely for another's sake."

"Well, my brother is interested in her and he's family, which will make her family. Sure, I'm an asshole, but family is family. She doesn't know what family means; I'm showing her."

"It looks more like you are showing her that death through a heart attack is a legitimate possibility." The angel's amusement helped, and my heart rate slowed to something a little saner.

Angels needed to visit Earth and laugh. The world would be a better place.

"Layla, in case no one has told you, angels are insufferable assholes, and they take a great amount of pride in this." Juan glared at the angel. "I'm asking for a favor, not a hard time."

"You amuse me." The angel stretched his wings, revealing blue and green bands of color on his feathers. "I can do as you ask. The answer may complicate matters, however."

"Everything is already complicated. There's an extensive art ring that's been using her for at least fifty years. She deserves a life, one that isn't made of prison walls and the profit of others. We have a theory about her possible heritage."

"As it is tiring to delve into the past or future, tell me what you can. I will then do the rest of the work as promised and fulfill my favor to you."

"Some sixty years ago, Layla was sold into the prison system and cultivated as an artist. There's no information in the records I found as to who sold her and why, but roughly every ten years, she would be released in such a way she would be reintroduced into the system, her previous identity lost. I suspect someone in the ring may have meddled with her memories to cover the transfers. She's been kept in severe ignorance of how the world works, if what I've been told is true."

"It's true," Dean said, and he scowled. "She was facing another life term for stealing a cupcake sprinkled with low-grade pixie dust. The proposed charges and desired punishment are what drew my attention to her file when I was searching the databases for someone interesting."

"She will keep life very interesting for you," the angel replied with laughter in his voice. "I do not even need to look into the future to see that. Tell me what you need from me, Juan."

"I want access to the best DNA scanner you can provide so we can get a full recording of her heritage, and I want you to tell us what you can of her family. We suspect she was stolen as an infant. She might be the descendant of a triad. We can't think of another way someone incarcerated so long among the worst North Carolina has to offer would stay so sweet. That's angelic genetics at play, in my opinion."

"Many humans have angelic origins," the angel replied. "Angels are what humanity could have been if things had only been a little different."

"Which divine should I thank that we're not?" Juan muttered.

The angel laughed. "Thank humanity itself. Humanity decided to be free. The DNA scanner and someone to operate it is an easy feat. The rest of what you ask will cover my debt in full. I lack the skills you require to delve into the shroud masking who and what she is. I am but a lesser angel, and someone has gone to great lengths to enshroud her and all she is—even from her. I cannot tell you what you will find when the shroud is torn away. For her, everything will change, and I cannot tell you what will remain of her when the truth of who she is comes to the surface. But you are right. She has had much stolen from her."

"Is her personality hers?" Dean demanded.

"The woman you love will remain the woman you love, but she will be able to access her potential. She will be changed in many ways, however. But change is change. It is neither good nor bad. How you handle the changes will decide your fates more than the existence changed. The shroud cannot take away everything, and the strongest facets of her personality shine through. You will find she is many things. The sweetness you treasure and the spirit burning bright are hers and have always been hers. But much of what she has lost will rise to the surface. The road will be long and frustrating, but the reward will be worth it should you decide to see things through."

My eyes widened. I'd been told my entire life that angels couldn't lie, and that the instant an angel told a falsehood, they would become twisted and fall, losing their status and power as an angel.

"That is true," the angel announced.

Despite the angel confirming what I'd been told, how could anyone love me? What had I done to deserve such a thing?

I barely knew Dean. He had no reason to love me.

"I wish you the best of luck with her, unicorn. You will need it. She is her greatest enemy in these things, and you will find yourself challenged throughout the years. You are equal to the task. What you will learn will bring change, and you will have many difficult choices to make moving forward. Is this what you want?"

I felt the angel's regard, and I wondered how a being without a head could stare at me with such intensity.

Every day of my life had involved doing what others had told me, following instructions without question, and being what others wanted me to be. Having a choice scared me almost as much the idea I would face the consequences of my choices for the rest of my life.

Until the angel had asked me, I hadn't realized freedom's weight could be as much of a burden as incessant time in a jail cell.

The angel shrugged. "That is the price of living as a free-willed being."

"I want to know." I expected disaster would come in the wake of my decision, but I would choose the cage I stayed in. I would still paint, but I would paint because I wanted to. I would see what the world could offer me. Even if the answer changed everything, I'd spent all of my time in prison dreaming of a world beyond the walls meant to keep me in. I'd spent my entire life painting a world I couldn't understand, especially without having a chance to live in it.

"Your sweetness, as your unicorn thinks of it, is the product of an angel's love for a human, but it was a very long time ago. Your mischief, such as it is, is the product of your darker heritage. But not all dark things are evil. You have wings to grow into, but they are not feathered for all they will be white."

"Can she be converted?" Dean asked, and his tone turned sharp.

"While unnecessary, yes. You will have no difficulty with her conversion."

"It is necessary!"

"Is this one of those overprotective stallion things, Xena?"

"Yes." Xena regarded the angel with narrowed eyes. "Can we stop dodging the issue here? What is she? Who are her parents? Was she actually stolen from her family when she was little? Are they still alive? What can you tell us about her? What sort of things will we need to do to protect her?"

"Some of those questions are easier to answer than others."

"Okay. What's the easiest of them to answer?"

"What she is would be the easiest, but that leads to answering a great many questions about how it is possible for her to be what she is. Also, answering if she was stolen should be simple enough. Which would you like for me to start with?"

"Start with if she was stolen. If so, Juan will have extra work on his plate."

"I already have a lot of extra work on my

plate. Stop adding to my work, Xena."

"No. You're the security specialist, so you have to do your security specialist duties. That means you have to do all the work for Layla. Dean might really try to kill you this time if you screw this up. He's invested."

"Yes, he's currently mentally impaired because of a mare he hasn't convinced to stick around. I'm aware."

Dean grunted. "You just want a round on the mat, don't you?"

Raising a brow, Juan faced off with Dean. "As a matter of fact, yes. It's been a few years since I've gotten to beat sense back into my little brother."

"Stop it, both of you," Xena ordered. "Juan, we all know you're going to work your best to protect her despite us all knowing she's going to kick ass and take names if anyone steps into her space without her permission. I'm convinced she can turn anything into a weapon."

"I know why that is," the angel announced. "Also, please think of me as Clarence. It is quite tiring being referred to as my species rather than my name. Right now, my name is Clarence. I am very aware I am an angel."

Oops. "I can't help it, it's your lack of a head. I see you are lacking a head, and I can't help but remember you're an angel, and then

I forget you have a name. I do appreciate you putting up with me, though."

"This is fair. Humans are so preoccupied with the presence of heads. But you are not truly human. You have been raised to be human, and a devil has gone out of his way to hide what you are. I find this annoying, truth be told."

Dean frowned. "A devil?"

"A minor one. It will be trivial enough for one of my brethren to remove the shroud and ensure it cannot be placed again. I cannot do it directly; I lack the finesse to leave her unharmed, but it will be done when she is ready. A few warnings, however."

If Clarence's goal was to confuse me, he succeeded. "What warnings? Why does that sound ominous?"

"It is not ominous. It would be best to prepare your unicorn for the reality of what removing the shroud will do."

"You are the most frustrating being I have ever met!" I gave my hair a yank. "It's like you're trying to be confusing and vague. Just say it!"

"You're a succubus."

Dean and Juan's eyes widened, and Xena covered her mouth with her hands. I blinked.

"A what?"

"Succubus. It's a type of demon who specializes in birth, reproduction, and pleasures of the flesh. Your stallion will enjoy many of the consequences of a relationship with you. Your heritage is coloring your existence in ways generally not seen in your ilk, however. You are strictly monogamous due to one of your grandmothers—well, several of them scattered throughout history. There are several divines playing a part in your existence, but I cannot see as clearly as other angels. I can sense your demonic energies even through the shroud. The shroud is suppressing most of your heritage, so only the strongest elements of your personality are currently shining through. Your temperament is a gift from a goddess who has long since left this coil, who loved one of the earliest humans. Their child is one of your grandfathers—if you added a few hundred generations between you and him. This emergence has brought many things long believed lost back to the surface. The shroud blocks some of my power, but the devil behind it lacked the foresight to shroud most of your ancestors. There is at least one triad in your ancestry. I can sense your angelic heritage as much as I can sense your demonic nature. I expect your demonic nature is leaking through the shroud because you are beginning to come into your power—and your power does wish to draw a suitable male. But your other ancestry would normally make it difficult for you to find a suit-able male. I expect your reaching power influenced your unicorn to come to you without him being aware he was being lured." The angel laughed. "A succubus ensnaring a unicorn. I have seen many things in my long life, but this is among the most amusing. A most unlikely partnership bound to bring chaos—and many new unicorns to the world. You will have to rein her in often, unicorn."

Dean scratched his head. "But she has ag-gressively defended herself from approaches from men."

"Yes. But I would not worry about her in-nocence. Her demonic nature will awaken when the shroud drops, and you will find yourself with a rather hungry and aggressive partner. You will want to give yourself several days of time to calm her, and even then, she will remain rather hungry and aggressive for several months until she is confident in binding you to her. It will be interesting for you."

Xena snickered. "You hear that, Dean? Clarence thinks you're going to have an in-teresting time with her."

"I hate you, Xena."

"He lies." Clarence laughed. "As for her love of art and her ability to paint, this is part of her demonic heritage. She is a creature of creation, and art is one of the ultimate forms of creation. I cannot tell you the why of that. I would have to examine the shroud closer, and I would rather my brethren do it in such a way as to not cause harm. When it is removed, it is possible to use our angelic influence to dampen the surge of demonic energy, but she will be on the hunt. She will need energy to sustain her lifeforce. Keeping her in a prison environment was likely chosen to give her energies she could harvest without being aware of it. Sexual tensions tend to be quite high."

"And she had to discourage men," Dean said through clenched teeth.

"Those very men she discouraged likely provided her with the energy she needed to survive. Once her powers awaken properly, she will need stronger energy to sustain her. Layla, the choice is yours on when the shroud should fall, but you will have much to learn. I would usually recommend another demon to teach you to control your powers, but you have a willing unicorn. He should suffice to calm your powers and meet your general demonic needs. After you have settled and staked your claim, a succubus could be requested to help you. You would be exceptionally young to grow your wings, but most would never restrain a fledgling demoness like you have been restrained. Should you have any surviving relatives, arrangements can be made. It's entirely possible you're the child of a succubus and incubus and were stolen from your parents, and one of them was descended from a human who developed demonic powers later in life. All I can tell is that you were not converted into a demoness. You were born one. And yes, a human may be converted into a demon just like you can be converted into a unicorn. It is a far different process, and it is often unpleasant at best. How would you like for me to proceed?"

Juan's cheek twitched, and he flexed his hands. Straightening his shoulders, he drew in a deep breath before exhaling. "Dean, we have a few days before Mom and Dad will have the herd here and be ready to act. If you want her, you need to want her as she is. Completely, aware of what she is, and the consequences of that. Also, I don't know if Mom is going to proud or horrified you want to cohort with a demon."

Dean flipped his middle finger at his brother. "But she's an amazing demon."

I rolled my eyes at that. "You hardly know me."

"I know everything I need to know to decide I would rather gamble on you than walk away. I don't even care if you lured me over. I want someone interesting, and that's exactly what I'll get with you. You have excellent taste in men, which is me."

"Are you crazy?"

"I'm a unicorn. I'm not crazy. I'm perfect."

Clarence laughed. "He is being quite honest with you."

"I suppose it would take a special brand of crazy to deal with me."

"It might take me an entire lifetime, but I fully intend on working with you until you believe there's nothing crazy about keeping you company, and that was before an angel told me you're a succubus."

"He is telling the truth."

"Why are you telling me he's telling the truth?"

"I am telling you because you need to know it is the truth, and that he is not just another male interested in having a night with a succubus."

"I don't want a night with a succubus. I want many nights with one very specific succubus, and if I need to be perfectly honest because there's an angel in the room, I'm having doubts my stallion virility will be able to keep up with her, and this was not something I was worried about this morning."

"Affection, the promise of offspring, and ready access to energy will keep a succubus around happily. We angels have a long history of participating in triads and keeping a demon or demoness content does involve a great deal of attention and affection. Succubi are easier to keep content, as they can be coaxed into staying to help care for their offspring. There are a few pairs from broken triads still together long beyond the death of their human, as bonds do form between angels and demons."

Dean's frown deepened. "That's going to be an issue considering how defensive of her territory and space she is."

"I am certain you will have no problems infiltrating her territory. The removal of the shroud will aid with that. I will go ask one of my brethren to look deeper into the situation, as there are angels far better than I at piercing such shrouds and delving into the secrets of the past."

Clarence disappeared in a flash of silvery light.

"Am I the only one completely weirded out by this whole thing?" I waved my hand to take in the hotel room, my excessive art supply question, and the questionable probability I'd landed in one hell of a mess. I struggled to come to terms with the reality I might be some form of demon.

I'd done questionable things over the years, but I hadn't thought I'd ranked anywhere close enough to be an evil minion of hell. Literally.

"I'm okay with this." Dean's expression smoothed, and he rubbed his hands together.

"Actually, the more I think about this, the happier I become. You won't have any problems protecting yourself, and I don't have any complaints about the various challenges I'll face having my very own succubus. You can be converted, and that's all I really care about."

Juan snickered. "You say that now, Dean. You haven't had a run in with a succubus before. She's going to wreck you. I've been with a friendly succubus who wanted to give a stallion a try. She wrecked me, and I did a good enough job she kept me company for a few weeks. The angel's right, though. Affection will keep a succubus around. They love to be loved, and the more you love her, the harder it'll be for her to wander off."

"I'm okay with this."

Xena grabbed a pillow and threw it at her brother. "You're a sick pervert."

"What? I'm a stallion, Xena. You know how we are. I'm not going to be ashamed of this. I wanted someone interesting when I began my search, and the lottery of life gave me a succubus. I'm the luckiest man alive. Not only do I get a succubus, the succubus is Layla, and she was already perfect before finding out she's a demoness."

"I'm hardly perfect."

"You are perfect. You just don't know it yet. I'm going to enjoy proving I'm right. I hope we have some spectacular arguments over it. I'm looking forward to the kissing and making up portion of these arguments. Xena, go get your own damned room."

Xena laughed. "I guess Mom and Dad would be okay with me staying with Juan for limited periods of time. Go get us a room, Juan. Then you can start doing more of that security work to figure out how we're going to make sure Layla is left alone. That ring goes down, and we're going to make sure no demons encroach on our turf. We haven't gone up against demons before. It'll be fun."

"Fun is not the word I'd use," Dean muttered.

"Sure it is. It's a challenge, and you get to show off for your lady in the process."

"He doesn't have to show off for me, Xena."

"You say that now, but trust me, there's nothing quite like a stallion showing off. When he does, enjoy yourself. He'll be spectacular. You could do a lot worse."

Scowling, Dean pointed at the door. "Go away."

Xena laughed, but she went to door as ordered. "Come on, Juan. We do not want to be here when the angels are done with Layla. There are some things I don't want to see, and my brother thoroughly losing his innocence to a succubus is one of them."

"Why aren't you worried about her innocence? You know full well I'm not a virgin, Xena. Just because we ultimately mate for life doesn't mean we start out that way. And don't you act like Mom isn't pressuring you to get some good experience, so you'll be a match for the stallion you tame. If you want an incubus, go hunt one and tame him."

Juan snickered. "Incubi don't tend to be loyal. Unless you're lucky, really good at taming one, or in league with an angel, you're not going to keep one around. Now, if you want to become a skilled lover for your stallion, hunt an incubus and present it that way. They love that sort of work. Hell, Mom's told all of us we should ensnare ourselves a succubus for a while. That Dean's going to keep his permanently will both please her and piss her off. It'll be great."

"Why will it piss her off?" I asked.

"It's simple, Layla. You're a demoness. We're unicorns. We're pretty much on the exact opposite spectrums. We're beings of purity despite our flexibility. You're anything but—although you're a black sheep among succubi from the looks of it. Maybe a white sheep, really."

Clarence and two angels with brilliantly banded wings in the colors of the rainbow popped into the suite, and silvery light flooded the room. When it faded, an incubus

joined them, and he lashed his tail. Unlike
Westin, the incubus resembled Dean, a
bronzed beauty of a man with dark hair that
complemented his jet black, leathery wings.
Something about the demon set me on edge,
and I reached for the nearest object I could
use as a weapon, one of the stacks of papers
on the coffee table.

Clarence caught my wrist. "Do not be
alarmed, Layla. He is a friend. More than a
friend, actually. His name is Emmanuel."

The angel's words only made my urge to
stab the incubus stronger, and I didn't even
care if the bastard had a nice name like
Emmanuel.

The demon laughed. "You weren't joking
about her coming into her wings early,
Clarence. I'm in her turf, and she's ready to
defend it. While I've enjoyed many a man,
Layla, I have no interest in yours. But the
pretty lady here is something special. I've
never enjoyed a unicorn before. Might you
know of an eligible mare who might want a
few nights with me?"

"No," Dean and Juan snapped.

Xena laughed. "That depends. Can I keep
you for a period of at least a month with a
sworn oath of no foals? We can reevaluate
after a month." Xena looked the incubus over.
"I bet you'd breed on command, and you'd be

able to encourage the formation of unicorn foals over humans."

"Indeed, I can. That said, I will have to decline your offer, only because it would make things somewhat awkward."

Xena scowled. "What do you mean by somewhat awkward?"

The incubus pointed at me. "I am her relative. And while I have enjoyed siblings before, the territorial stallion would be upset. While I'm a demon, I am not a splitter of homes and families. This goes against everything my line believes."

I narrowed my eyes. "You're a what of mine?"

"Relative. We are bound by familial blood. Clarence requested help in repaying his debt, and Paul looked into the past through the shroud and traced your lineage to me. They felt I was the best choice of the available demons and devils to handle this matter. They're probably right. You'll need to be prepared to meet the rest of the family, and I'm the least... frightening."

One of the angels, likely the one named Paul, waved. Unlike Clarence, his wings were banded in the colors of the rainbow, although he had an extra band of blue in his pattern, unlike his fellow angel, who had an extra band of yellow.

The incubus's statement didn't sound

promising. "If you're trying to piss me off, it's working."

Dean laughed, came close, and peeled Clarence's hand off my wrist. "Wait to attack him until after you hear what he has to say, and should you need to get violent, keep it non-lethal. Blowing off some steam would probably do you some good, but pick a better target. I understand why you're frustrated, however. Everything's been changed on you."

"For a unicorn, you're quite tolerant of violence," the incubus complained.

"My species goes onto battlefields and eats the dead to prevent the spread of disease and ensure passage to the afterlife. Violence is a part of who we are. And we are not against the use of violence to protect our own. Should you hurt Layla, I will enjoy crushing you to paste and returning your soul to the darkest pit in the nastiest hell I can find."

"I see you've been ensnared rather heavily. You're going to have to watch for that, Layla. It will be quite easy for you to enthrall men. It's something you will actively have to control. Now, of course, if you wish to keep this male for a while, you're doing a very good job of securing him. If he gets much more interested, you're going to have to restrain him until you're ready to enjoy him. That shroud will be a problem. It's doing a lot more than suppressing your demonic abilities." The incubus wrinkled his nose and looked me over from head to toe. "Paul, can you add a dampener of your own that can fade on its own over a period of, say, six months? That should be long enough for her to adapt to her powers without killing her unicorn. She's too young to be developing this quickly, but I suspect it's because of the shroud. The human elements of our heritage and breed are advancing her long before her time. Usually, our kind develops over a period of a few hundred years. You're not even a hundred yet."

"So, her being in her sixties is correct?" Dean asked.

"She was born during the emergence, and she was stolen while the first wave of magic brought chaos into the world. Unless I'm mistaken, she was the first child born of this emergence."

"She is," Clarence confirmed. "That is part of why I had difficulty seeing the truth of her past. That much magic converging on Earth makes our vision blurred. Paul helped. She is eighty-six. Should you wish to learn more about her altered development, Emmanuel can help you."

"It will be my pleasure. And it will be the pleasure of our family to help bring an end to those who have done this to us. As such, we formally request an exemption from the rules of our war to deal with this matter. I would rather not anger *Him* over a personal matter."

"*He* will pay no heed to this as long as you target only those who have played a role in this event," Paul announced. "*He* has also granted us leave to aid you as we can. This will clear our debt to Juan and balance the scales for all the times your lines have helped ours."

"We will consider all debts repaid," Emmanuel replied.

"Then we're agreed. Our ability to act will be limited by *His* will, but we will not interfere with your activities. Should a greater devil be involved, we will need to know, but we will turn away from such activities."

"Warring factions of devils are responsible for this, although Layla is no longer of interest to most devilish entities. Her father, of course, is interested, but the shroud hides her from his sight. That is the true purpose of the shroud: not to prevent her from knowing what and who she is, but to prevent her father from finding her. The devil who stole her has paid already, but our family was unable to find her. We did look. We still do."

The angels stilled, and Clarence clamped his wings close to his back. The other two relaxed, and something in the room changed. A weight lifted from my shoulders, one I hadn't realized I'd carried.

"He speaks the truth," the unnamed angel said, breaking the heavy silence. "*He* loathes when families are broken by pointless feuds and wars. And for all the hosts of Heaven and Hell wage war, it is not a war to be waged by our offspring, not until the End of Days. And for all she is a demon, *He* has seen her heart and has judged it worthy."

"I should be disgusted, but I am unsurprised. That would be my great-grandmother's doing. You can't have a goddess who represents love and life in its entirety in a bloodline without having the rare black sheep in a devilish and demonic family."

Damn it, at the rate we were going, I'd never get a straight answer out of anyone. "Could you assholes stop being so vague and just tell me who you are, what's going on, and why you're even here?"

"My name is Emmanuel, and your mother is my sister, a succubus who has wed one of Satan's lieutenants. The feud between the devils resulted in your kidnapping shortly after your birth. You are the first demon born of this emergence period. Until the shroud is removed, I won't be able to tell which powers of your ancestry have awoken, but I expect you'll have your fair share of all your heritage. Power tends to grow strong in the first born of every race during an emergence. Your loss was a great blow to my sister and the devil she wed. Their vengeance has changed the very face of all the devil's hells."

"He speaks the truth," Clarence said. "You are a wanted child, and *He* knows this. This is part of why *He* is willing to cooperate. *He* does not like when families are broken."

"*He will* outgrow that one of these days," Emmanuel replied, his tone amused. "*He* still grows into his portfolio. Give *Him* a hundred years. *He* will be as much of an asshole as any angel."

The angels laughed.

I frowned. "Isn't that going to offend *Him*?"

"*He* is not so easily offended," Clarence replied. "Ours is a twisted family. But you are not any relatives of ours, although there is an angel in your ancestry. Once the shroud drops, he will know his offspring's offspring's offspring's offspring has had a child and you were hidden from him. He will show. That is his nature. He will show angry and ready to wage war, but that is his nature. That is why Paul and Derek have both come. They will be able to prevent any unfortunate misunderstandings when he arrives. I do recommend that you take care, Emmanuel. He will be enraged upon his arrival."

"I understand that well enough. Rage over this has been something we have long endured. Anyway, I'm one of those offspring's offspring's offspring or however many off-springs it is, so he won't flip at me. I make no promises about anyone else in the room. I'll get a hug." Emmanuel smirked. "And you'll all be upset because he won't hug you."

"You are a terrible demon," Clarence muttered.

"Yes, I'm so terrible for having an affectionate great-great-grandfather. That's the problem with angels. Once they join the family, you just can't get rid of them. I really need to ask my great-great-grandmother what she was thinking joining with an angel."

Paul laughed. "She loved him, and he loved her enough to conspire with a demon to produce children. That is how these things work. But, we should return to the subject at hand, as we are confusing your niece, who does deserve the truth of this matter. Once we drop the shroud, this room will become very crowded. Her father will surely show, and he will bring her mother, and the angels of her line will also arrive."

My eyes widened. "Angels is plural. There's more than one?"

"You have six angels in your line. They are all named."

Something about Paul's statement chilled me. "Named?"

"Michael. Gabriel. Lucifer before his fall. These are only three of the named angels.

They are not the angels of your line. Lucifer
has never birthed any children and cannot. It
is a price of his power, just like *He* can no
longer have any children, although *His* child's
portfolio passes from human to human every
emergence. Right now, *His* child's portfolio
slumbers. The previous holder of the portfolio did not hold it long before it fled him.
He proved unworthy."

Emmanuel frowned. "The portfolio fled?"

"Less it fled, more that it was an echo of
what it should have been. We do not know
who possesses the portfolio now—or if the
portfolio will reawaken this emergence.
Times have changed. *He* only smiles when we
ask *Him*, as even we are blocked from the future's secrets. *His* next child already pleases
Him. Which worries us."

"Why does that worry you?" I asked.

"*He* enjoys when the unexpected comes to
Earth. As Emmanuel said, *He* has not yet fully
grown into *His* portfolio. Truth be told, we
hope *He* remains as *He* now is. This change
has been good for this Earth. It gives us hope
the End of Days will take longer arriving.
Nothing is eternal, but all beings wish to continue to exist, even us angels. I suspect *His*
next child is not a son but a daughter, which
would match well to the devil having a
daughter of the spirit if not of the body. This
emergence, it appears as though women will

change the world. This is not a bad thing. Men have dominated most of humanity's history. We shall see what comes of change."

"Terror," Juan muttered. "Women are terrifying creatures."

Dean laughed. "I can't say he's wrong. Our mother is most certainly a terrifying creature."

"I'm doing both of you idiots a favor. I won't tell Mom you said that. You owe me."

The brothers sighed.

"Could we please lay this out for me in a clear and concise manner, one that doesn't require me to use math or spell anything, please?"

"We can help you with the knowledge you were denied in your youth," Paul replied. "Modifying your memories so you have the knowledge of basic written language and mathematics is within our capabilities. Usually, we allow humans to learn such things on their own, but this impairment is too significant for the other challenges you face. It will be done after we remove the shroud and handle the aftermath of so many upset beings teleporting into the same space. I suspect your grandfather will wish to handle your lost education. Also, please do just address him as your grandfather. It gets complicated trying to track the number of generations."

"Okay. This won't offend him?" I asked,

not sure how anyone would want to be addressed like that by me without having met me before.

"No. It will not. Angels take family very seriously. He will call you his granddaughter with pride because you are proof the woman he once loved had lived. She is long gone from this Earth. Her seed of life has yet to be replanted, but I expect she will find herself with a winged lover in her next future. For now, she rests safe in *His* care. Some souls have active afterlives, some slumber. She rests for now. While your grandfather is willing to wage war without hesitation, his love is equal to his aggression. He is one of the more aggressive angels, a general of *His* army. That is why there will be trouble for a time. A lieutenant of the hells and a general of *His* army in the same room will be entertaining for some of us."

Emmanuel raised his hand. "I will be very amused."

"You will also have to keep your grandfather from attempting to slaughter your brother-in-law."

"I'm not worried about it. Elize will be crying and trying to cuddle with Layla, and I suspect my niece will not react well, there will be a fight, and it'll be chaos. Her father's parenting instincts will kick in, and he'll recognize Layla is his descendant and try to calm the situation. If you could try to resist murdering your parents when they come into your space, that would be appreciated. That instinct is your father's fault, and he'll be able to teach you how to control it. You do that because you have no idea how to distinguish friend from foe, so you eject everyone from your space." Emmanuel grinned, and he rubbed his hands together. "Do make sure your dampeners are good, Paul. She'll have a lot of rogue instincts we'll have to teach her how to control."

"I will make the dampeners last a period of three years with a gradual decay," Paul replied, "Six months will not be sufficient with her heritage, and we would not wish for her to damage her male in her enthusiasm."

Dean sighed. "I'm going to be Layla's male in this family, aren't I?"

"Yes," the angels and the incubus replied.

I laughed. "Your family seems determined to call me your mare. We're even now. If you take me to the art store again to look around, I'll suggest they should call you my stallion."

"You don't even need to negotiate that. If you want to go to the art store, I'll take you to the art store."

I wasn't sure what to say to that, and of my options, I picked Xena as the one most likely to offer somewhat reasonable advice on how to react.

Xena smiled. "Just say thank you."

"Thank you, Dean."

"You're welcome. If you would like to hide behind me for the initial chaos, I should be able to withstand a few cranky angels, a devil, and whatever else shows up when the shroud drops."

"Perhaps you should transform first," Emmanuel suggested. "Even a devil hesitates to attack a unicorn, especially when there are other unicorns in the room. Unicorns have a reputation."

That sounded interesting. "They do? What sort of reputation?"

"They hold grudges for longer than most beings, and they are willing to use the weapon attached to their head whenever they're annoyed. Unicorns decided long ago they weren't going to participate in the war between law and chaos or good and evil. They also decided they'd bang heads together on both sides if necessary. That's why they're battlefield shepherds. They're neutral more than anything. The whole nonsense about them being pure beings is just that: nonsense. They just look pure and innocent until they're hungry."

"I was warned they had special dietary requirements."

"Once the shroud drops, you will not find their special dietary requirements a bother. If anything, you'll like it. Your heritage makes a matter of souls serious to you, and it'll appeal to you to shepherd souls to their proper destinations despite needing to take a nibble or two from the body. Your devilish ancestry will make it so you have other tricks to dispose of the bodies and perform your other duties post conversion. And, should your male expire prematurely, you can shake off the conversion at your will."

Dean frowned at that news.

"I can shake it off?"

"You're a blend of devil, demon, angel, and a lot of other things. If you've got access to your angelic powers, you'll be able to purge your new unicorn DNA without issue. That's an angelic ability. You might even be able to teleport in time."

"Okay, Dean. I have to give you some credit. You've gone and gotten yourself ensnared by one hell of a woman." Xena giggled. "I can't wait until Mom finds out you're dating a daughter of the heavens and hells."

Derek pressed the palms of his hands together and held his hands close to his chest as though he prayed. "Actually, she is more like a daughter of Hell. She was just born on Earth because a new demonic seed of life became available to the Lord of Lies. He rewarded his lieutenant, Layla's father, with the seed. Had no seeds been available, she would have been born a human. But *He* offered *His* fallen angel a new seed. That is kin to giving him a new child. *He* forged a new angel that day, too. I suppose you can consider them sisters. She was the first angel born of this emergence, too."

"What does that mean for me?" I asked.

"Very little. You are a demon, but the Lord of Lies offers his demons many freedoms. It is his nature. You have the free will to do as you please. When the End of Days comes, it will become a battle like none other, and demons, devils, and angels will have to decide what roles they play. There is no record of what must be during the End of Days. Nobody knows except *Him*, and those are secrets *He* will hold until all has been lost and the seeds of life are planted anew, and the cycle begins again. But it seems those days will be a long time in coming. You will be able to enjoy your life as you want with your stallion, have your children as you want, and live. I will not tell you if any of your children will become demons, devils, or angels. Some things are best left discovered naturally."

"I like that you used the word children. Children is plural." Dean grinned. "I don't want a number. Knowing there will be more than one is good enough for me."

The angels snorted, and Derek replied, "You will wed a succubus, and they are simply unhappy if they do not have their offspring around. As soon as you get rid of one, you will have another, and truth be told, it won't be long after they have learned some independence, she will desire another child. You will have many foals, and it will be rare times you do not have one, two, or even ten running around at your feet causing you trouble."

My brows shot up at the thought of having more than one child around while Dean kept grinning. "I like this math," he replied.

Juan shook his head and sighed. "You are even worse than Dad."

"There's nothing wrong with Dad. He loves Mom, and he's always loved us. Dad is a most excellent example of a good father."

"He speaks the truth," Clarence announced.

Well, that was something. I couldn't stop my jealousy from surging, but I did my best to ignore it. "And my father?"

Emmanuel snickered. "Your stallion will be kept busy making sure your family doesn't take you into custody without him. Devils are not usually all that skilled with social grace when it comes to their offspring's partners. I'll try to remind your parents you'll be more comfortable if they take your stallion along for the trip, too. Especially as you grow more into your powers, you'll probably get rather unhappy to be separated from him. My sister gets very irritable when she's separated from her mate. Once a succubus bonds and wants to stick around, good luck getting rid of her. Incubi like me don't tend to bond as readily, but we can figure out the loyalty thing under the right conditions—or if we have an angelic slave driver around keeping us on the straight and narrow."

The angels snickered, and Clarence stretched out his wing and smacked Emmanuel with it. "You would be among the first incubi approached for a triad, and you know this."

"I like threesomes a lot."

"Of course you do. You're an incubus," the angel muttered. "If you had your way, every day would be a public orgy."

"This is true. Threesomes make dedication worth it, and there's little as enjoyable for us as having our way with an angel."

Some things I didn't want to know. Listening to someone who was supposedly my uncle flirt with an angel ranked fairly high in things I didn't want to do. "Please stop. I don't care if you want to go bang an angel, but please do so where I'm not forced to listen to it."

Emmanuel laughed. "Well, that's all the evidence I need that you're definitely going to be the white sheep of the family. If your wings come in white to match your unicorn, I'll be amused. I'll also enjoy taunting my sister about her unique daughter. We'll have a good time, especially if we offend your stallion. Unicorns are great entertainment when offended. If we stole you off to one of the pits of hell for a visit, he'd storm the place to get you back."

"Yes, I would. Please don't. I would become covered in soot. Do you know how hard it is to remove soot stains?"

"Soot is a good look on me. So is a pretty woman. Angels are even better on me." Emmanuel leered at Paul. "Find yourself a human lady and pay me a visit. I'll keep you both company."

"Heaven help me," the angel replied. "What did I do to deserve that?"

"I want to taste your rainbow."

Wow. I opened my mouth, closed it, and frowned, not sure how to handle being related to a shameless pervert.

"You will be a shameless but dedicated pervert within three years, so try not to be too upset with your uncle," Paul said. "You will get used to it. As far as incubi go, he is a friendly one. He is a good candidate for a triad despite his perversions. He is dedicated to his offspring and will not create new offspring until his are fully grown. To his standards, fully grown tends to be his offspring's entire lifespan. He has only had human children, as he has not been granted a new seed, and he does not wish demonic offspring enough to take one from a more ambitious demon."

"Can we go back to beating art counterfeiters? I'm much more comfortable with that conversation."

"That is your father in you. He's much more comfortable with violence than affection. Your mother has worked wonders with him, but he does still prefer a good fight."

I could only think of one response, and it made me a bad person. "Dean, can I smash his nose into your skull? The longer he talks, the more I want to break his nose on your head."

Dean laughed. "Don't beat up your uncle, Layla. While it's tempting, he's part of your family."

Helpless over how to handle the situation, I turned to Xena for help.

"Don't look at me, Layla. I have an entire herd of relatives. Once that shroud drops, it will be chaos."

"Can I run away now?"

"No, but you can hide behind me. First, we reclaim your family. After you have a chance to meet them and my family, we'll go beat those who are responsible for your mistreatment. I plan on enjoying it, and I don't

care if I ruin the reputation of the entire unicorn race in the process."

"He means that," Clarence said.

Dean meant a lot of what he said, something I'd figured out without the angel's help.
"Am I reclaiming them, or are they participating in a hostile invasion? I'm not sure I
want to deal with a hostile invasion. They
might damage my painting supplies."

"That's a good point. Emmanuel, I don't
suppose you can do the responsible thing and
call her parents so there isn't a feud in the
room? Those supplies are treasures to her
and damaging them or her painting would
upset her." Dean narrowed his eyes. "I will
have an issue if she is upset because her work
is damaged."

"I have seen a lot of things in my long life,
and I'm ashamed to admit I'm concerned over
what you will do if you have an issue."

"That depends on how upset she
becomes."

If I let the unicorn do whatever he
wanted, I worried there'd be bodies—bodies
he would eat. "You don't have to do that,
Dean."

"I don't have to, but I'll certainly enjoy it.
If it makes you happy, I'll present their heads
on a silver platter for you."

"Why silver? I always wanted to know
why everyone wants to bring things to others

on a silver platter. Why not a gold one? Or some other metal?"

"Stainless steel just seems so sterile."

I groaned, as did everyone else in the room.

"What?"

Emmanuel grunted, dug into the pocket of his form-fitting suit, and retrieved his phone. "Do you want me to call Grandfather, or will you explain the situation to him?"

Paul sat on the edge of the couch cushion, careful to keep his wings close to his back. "He will want to remove the shroud himself should we warn him. This is not a bad thing. He would be gentle with her. I will insist I handle placing the dampeners. I have more finesse than he does. I will take care of it."

The angel disappeared in a flash of silvery light.

"I'll step out into the hallway for this, but they'll show up sooner than later. They've been waiting for this day for a long time. Try not to worry, Layla. Everything will work out. Oh, and Dean?"

"Yes?"

"If you hurt her, I will be picking out pieces of your fur from my teeth for years." Emmanuel left the room.

At a complete loss of what to do, I did the one thing I still knew: I painted.

ELEVEN

Don't you even think about testing
that stallion.

AT THE RATE beings kept popping into the
hotel room, we'd run out of room for everybody. I took over the corner to the window
with my hoard of paints and canvases, creating the equivalent of a cell to keep everyone
out of my space.

It seemed a lot safer to stay in my corner
than mingle with others.

As though somehow sensing I'd reached
my limit, Dean transformed and stood guard,
blowing air and stomping his hooves whenever anyone tried to approach. His snorts,
few and far between, promised violence if his
warnings weren't heeded.

Emmanuel laughed. "Well, she's definitely
tamed that stallion. He's going to go for
someone's throat soon enough trying to keep
everyone out of her territory."

"Painting is how she copes with things,"

Xena replied. "When she's upset, she'll go right to her art supplies and fiddle with them. And if she's really unbalanced, she'll start painting. She was happiest in the art store, but she was also shocked by how much we bought for her. I went a little crazy there. If she showed interest in it, I got her the best stuff I could find. I think they were using custom pigments for her paintings, as they weren't in branded bottles or tubes. She hasn't complained about the quality. Her sketch of Dean is incredible, though. She was going to make me pose for her, but she fixated on my brother and seems determined to use only him as her model right now."

"That's normal," my uncle replied. "Succubi fixate. Young succubi who are more inclined to bond fixate the most. Normally, she would start fixating after a hundred or so, but she's advanced for her age. If she'd been raised with us, she would have started hunting men to learn the trade at fifty, but she'd be treated as a regular woman; her full powers wouldn't develop until a little later. That's good, as she needs time to adjust anyway. And Elize, don't you even think about testing that stallion. When Layla is ready to come out, she'll come out. I know you want to go cuddle, but you're just going to have to wait."

A woman sniffed. "I'm satisfied he has her interests at heart."

"You're satisfied he has her interests at heart because you're a shameless succubus using your empathic abilities to track him. You're also making your shameless hussy of a husband read his thoughts and tell you what he's thinking. You're probably having him read your daughter, too, to keep a close eye on her."

"As a matter of fact, yes. Privacy is an illusion when there are angels and devils around."

I could only assume the woman was my mother, and I debated if I was ready to put away my paint brushes and face my new reality.

Yesterday, my mother had been a woman who'd wanted to drown me and had ditched me in prison for profit.

Today, my mother was a demoness who'd partnered with a devil, and I wasn't sure what I thought about that.

In a normal person's life, the humans would have been the better beings. In mine, the lines blurred until I couldn't tell who belonged on which side. Even the angels seemed to have motivations beyond doing good.

"You are wise beyond your years," Clarence said. "Angels are considered to be beings of good, but through the eyes of others, we are anything but. Two archangels wiped three cities from the world for the greater good. They saved those they could, but they brought death and grief to many. To those they hurt, angels are anything but good. Those would rather dance with the devil than see another angel. Through your eyes, no one can be trusted, except perhaps the stallion you fixate on because he has shown you justice in little ways and picked your side without knowing anything about you. His decision to spit on that attorney sealed his fate."

"I spit on that bastard, too. He deserved it. He deserves a lot more than spit in the face."

"There are two demons and a devil in the room who will be quite pleased to make sure he gets a lot more than spit in the face." Clarence laughed, and I relaxed at the sound. "Justice will come, and she will witness it. I do not foresee her doing much more than witnessing what is to come, but it will work out for the best. Some things are written in the stars, and I see no other fate for those who have stirred the wraths of the many hells and even the heavens."

"I have an extended family," a man said, and his words rumbled in his chest. "I am debating how many of the family I should call in—or if I should reach higher."

I could only assume the man was my father; he'd been silent since his arrival, although I'd heard Emmanuel greet him. I debated peeking, but I decided I preferred working on painting Dean's mane. Painting the shades of pale gray and silver that brought the white of his coat to life took a great deal of concentration.

Once I beheld my parents, everything would change again, and I would have to evaluate every day of my life and rewrite my past, identifying every lie that had led to the person I'd become.

Some mountains I didn't want to climb. What would remain?

Paul dared to approach, and he gave Dean's shoulder a companionable slap before stepping into my domain. I considered stabbing the angel with my paintbrush, but I realized I actually liked the angel and didn't mind him entering my territory. He stood behind me and watched me work.

"If you reach higher, you will find things will resolve faster, and she will have more time to process everything that has happened. More importantly, she will see the true meaning of justice. Your family has already paid its dues, and she has no true idea what it means to have those who will stand with her and with you. That leads me to the matter of the shroud. Should I do the work, I can help heal some of what has been done. I will link my work to the dampeners. As her power grows, the principles and lessons she should have learned young will be absorbed and blend with all you teach her moving forward. She has lost much, and this would balance all debts owed. It is rare we can do so much direct good for a single soul, and it would be an honor to undo some of the damage done to an innocent. And that is what she is, a reality you must face. For all she has inherited many of your tendencies, she is still a creature of innocence. I am not sure how much of that will change. That is a future I have not checked, nor will I. I would rather she choose her future than try to mold her future based on one possibility."

"Then I will reach higher. How high should I go?"

"*He* has already involved *Himself* in this, and it would do well to maintain the balance."

Paul's statement ushered in a deep silence, and I broke it rattling my paint brush in the cleaning tin. "I always wondered if the Devil was as scary as people seem to believe. I always wondered if God was a scary as people seem to believe, too. I could never tell which one was worse in prison. God was treated as a tool of salvation, but I never saw any god come into prison to save anybody. And they'd blame the Devil for what they did, and that never seemed fair to me. And what's this nonsense about putting the fear of the Devil —or God—into people? It's not like either really comes to pay a visit to anybody."

"You are much more likely to meet the Devil than you are to meet *Him*, truth be told," Paul admitted, and he patted my shoulder. "You can meet both if you would like. *He* is willing to bear witness. *He* knows you will never be one of *His* children; you will always be what you are, no matter how pure your spirit is. But just as there have always been angels who fall from grace, there are always demons and devils who rise above their lot in life. Some might say the Devil is one of those."

The angels snickered.

"I feel like I have missed something."

"The relationships of the denizens of the highest heavens and the darkest depths of the hells are complicated. Angels and devils alike are capable of hatred and love of equal measure, and that colors the nature of our war, as it always has. After all, the Devil was once a beloved child of the heavens and in many ways, he still is. Ours is a strange family. You will learn this soon enough. You will find you also have a patient family. That is one of the benefits of belonging to a long-lived race. No one can return your lost childhood, but you will find your first steps into your adulthood will be full of light and love.

And sulfur. An unfortunate amount of sulfur."

Dean whipped his head around and snapped his teeth at Paul.

"Your stallion is upset that he has to share you with the rest of your family. He wants to be the one to exclusively adore you for the rest of your days. You are just going to have to accept others showing her affection. She will find your skirmishes with her parents amusing, so do posture for her enjoyment. You should be happy she has fixated enough she views you as her safe haven already."

My mother laughed, and while she couldn't brighten the entire room with her amusement, I found the sound to be comforting.

The woman I'd believed to be my mother had never laughed, and it offered hope that I wouldn't make a mess of everything.

Once she finished chuckling, my mother said, "It is quite all right, Paul. We can share her with young Dean. It is good for her to have a man she can trust even though he will test her shapeshifting abilities. It is usually centuries before a young succubus masters the art of shapeshifting. She hasn't mastered another form yet. There's no need to rush her into anything. She's been rushed enough. It's enough knowing she's safe. Removing the shroud will change everything for her."

"It will change everything for you, too."

"Yes," my mother agreed. "Can I greet her grandfather with my fist?"

Paul laughed. "Of course. He's your grandfather. You can do whatever you want to him. He has always enjoyed your rather violent greets."

"Dean, why is everyone so weird?"

Dean whinnied and bobbed his head.

"He wishes for me to tell you that it took weird people to make someone as special as you," Paul translated.

"You're hopeless, Dean."

"He certainly is. Are you ready for the shroud to be broken, Layla? When I do this, you will enter a trance. During the trance, I will revive your true memories, set the dampeners, and evaluate your life from the moment you were taken to now. It will be intrusive, but I will be able to accurately glean the identities of the guilty doing so. You will be aware of everything I see, as I will not hide my presence from you. The important things, I will disclose on your behalf, as it is probable you are unable to identify what is of importance."

"That's fair."

"It will not be comfortable, but you are used to uncomfortable things. I will also help you be able to adapt to so many changes at once. These aids will fade along with the dampeners. Most importantly, you will be able to handle physical contact easier. This is a matter of your past environments. While I will not erase those memories, I will make it easier for you to identify friend from foe and react less violently towards those you wish to show affection to. Unless, of course, you wish to break your uncle's nose upon your stallion's head. I am sure your parents would reward you well for such things, as they are twisted people."

Emmanuel laughed. "Every time she looks at me, she really does think about doing that, too. It amuses me. From the instant I stepped into her territory, she's wanted to get rid of me. My sister wanted to kill me from birth, too. I have yet to figure out why the women in my life want to kill me."

"Good sense. She recognizes an idiot when she sees one," my mother replied.

"I'm hurt, Elize."

"You're incapable of being hurt. Stop being a baby. Also, if you raise a finger to my little girl, I will rip your fingers off and shove them up your ass."

"Ouch. What did I do to deserve that?"

"You obviously annoyed my little girl, and you should suffer as a result."

"Dean wishes me to tell you he now understands where you get some of your tendencies, and it is not from your father as he believed," Paul said.

"I'm far more interested in actions than words, and I accept all responsibility for her inclination to beat offensive beings without warning," my father said.

I had a family, and they were crazier than I was. That would take some getting used to. "How did you become the sane one, Dean?"

Dean whinnied, stretched towards me, and brushed his nose against my cheek.

"Hey, what about me?" Xena asked.

"You want to take over the world. You don't get to make any claims to sanity."

"Oh. Right. That's fair. Can we hurry this show up? I want to see how many angels we can cram into a room at the same time. If we're lucky, it'll be an explosion of feathers, and that will be fucking hilarious. I'm going to record it, and I'm going to upload it to the internet, and I'm going to use all the profits to fund my world domination efforts."

Knowing Xena, she really would. "I will break your phone on your thick skull if you take any videos with me in it."

"I would resent that, except I would totally earn it, and you were even nice enough to warn me where the line was. I will make certain I do not record you. Dean, however, is fair game."

While my skills with math needed a lot of

work, some concepts I understood. "If you use Dean, you will pay me half of the money you earn so I can buy art supplies."

"Wow. You're ruthless. Fine. I accept your terms, but your angelic relatives better put on a good show."

I would never understand Xena. "I'm technically not related to you no matter what I do with Dean, right?"

"You would become my sister."

"But will your crazy infect me?"

Xena sighed. "No, it won't. But Dean's plenty crazy, and his special brand of crazy really will."

Some prices were worth paying. I shrugged. "Okay."

"You'll accept his crazy but not mine? That's not fair at all!"

"I like him more than I like you."

"In your shoes, I'd like him more than I like me, too. Okay. You win this round, but I sure hope these angels put on a good show. I need to be entertained."

As I had no idea what would come, how long the warned trance would last, or if chaos in the form of angels would sweep through the room, I took my time putting my art supplies away properly, and I put my painting of Dean in the corner hoping it would be spared from harm. Once I finished, I braced myself for what would come, and said, "Okay. I'm ready."

Paul crouched in front of me and took hold of my hand. "I will take my time and be as gentle as possible, and when I am finished, you will feel much better. I promise."

Fool that I was, I believed him.

BY TRANCE, Paul had actually meant private torture session within the confines of my own head. Somehow, the angel forced me to relive my entire life, but at a certain point, things went sideways. It didn't hurt, not really, but confusion reigned.

Then, the chaos settled, and Paul guided me through my own life with a steadying touch.

I hadn't been wrong. Every time I'd enjoyed a taste of freedom, I'd been paid a visit by a devil, and he'd masked his presence in my memories. In my reversing memory, the first five devils I'd met were one and the same, a dark creature enshrouded in flame with a gentle touch and a twisted sense of humor.

I hadn't remembered, but he'd bought me tea and cake, he'd made me laugh, and he made the same promise Paul had: soon, things would become better.

Like with Paul, I'd believed that devil.

Then time turned back a little further, and a new devil took the other's place, one who inspired fear and erased all the good things in my life with tedium, art, and a past that was nothing more than an illusion.

I'd never had a mother who'd tried to drown me. While I did receive cards, there'd been no father behind them.

Instead, I'd been fed by a devil who cared nothing for me, left with crayons and paper to amuse myself, and given the minimal care. To encourage my interest in the arts, that devil had surrounded me with pretty pictures, and the times I'd tried to mimic them with my crayons, I'd been praised.

I'd drank up that little praise, and I'd fixated on the one thing I could to do earn any approval at all.

And I'd done well at it.

Some of my memories were the truth; I'd entered the prison system at age five, but not in the way I'd believed. I'd been sequestered alone, left to paint and praised whenever I accomplished something profitable. When I'd turned eight, the earliest I could make a more permanent stay in a correctional facility for children, I'd been given a record, and I'd been set loose hungry so that record could be given weight.

The rest of my life had gone as I'd explained to the court, and my ignorance had been as much of a cage as the stone walls and cold cells of prison.

Here and there, Paul showed me a memory, but rather than leave it be, he did something, something that explained a mystery of life. Through my own struggles, he planted seeds of knowledge, ones that grew to a stronger understanding of everything I'd been denied in my youth.

Then, before he retreated from my memories, he guided me to the very beginning, piercing the distance haze to one of my mother and my father cooing over me, holding me, and showering me with their affection in the first days of my life.

Paul's laughter drew me from my memories. A shower of feathers rained down, someone squawked, and Xena laughed. Angels and their wings took up a lot of space, and the newcomers tripped over each other, confusion reigned, and the gentle devil from my newer memories rubbed Dean's nose.

One of the stallion's ears turned back, but he tolerated the attention.

"You gave me cake, but then you took the memory."

"It was necessary. The time wasn't right, but I wanted to forge a connection. That requires exposure. I knew it was only a matter of time before my plans would come to fruition, but your heritage awakening early would've spoiled the workings in progress. Isn't he a lovely specimen?"

"Why are you petting Dean?"

"I like unicorns. They amuse me. The white ones are masters of deceit, and I appreciate such things. This one is stunning, isn't he?"

"Instead of putting your hands all over my unicorn, you should bring me some more of that cake. You're the reason I made a fool of myself over a pixie dust cupcake, aren't you?"

"My cakes did help a little, but those cakes were special. They contained more than sugar and spice and everything nice. They were infused with demonic essence, the same kind that sustains succubi."

Paul chuckled. "I had wondered about how she'd emerged from such a life so unscathed. You'd been sustaining her. More openly in later years."

"I've been providing for many years, slipping in unseen or sending a possessed human into the system to ensure she was sustained. Part of her advanced maturity is my fault. I couldn't act openly quite yet, and it's very difficult to manage the dosage of energies. It's worked well. Her unicorn would have been unhappy if she'd emerged from captivity starved. She'll have a chance to adapt to feeding herself, and he'll have a chance to adapt to being her primary provider. Anyway, some of my devils are slower than others at revenge. I'm talking about your sire. His desire for revenge came second only to his love for his wife and child. He's been delightful, making a mess of every hell he could worm his way into on his quest for revenge."

"You're an asshole," my father snarled.

"Yes, I am. Admit it. You're secretly pleased I safeguarded your child. You'll forgive me in a few decades. The time wasn't right, and you'd worked so hard for quality revenge. And your revenge? It was a work of art. You might say I've shown you my favor this way. You destroyed one of my generals, and had I been home attending to that matter rather than flitting around the mortal coil, you would have been robbed of such satisfying destruction. As you destroyed one of my generals, you'll just have to clean up your mess and take his place. Such a tragedy. You certainly gathered enough support among even demons. You'll have more demonic soldiers than devilish one, but this will be your strength."

More feathers fell around me, and I caught one, a large one with a velvety texture. "Can I use these to make a pillow?"

The devil who'd earned my father's wrath chuckled. "Sure. If those pesky angels wanted to keep their feathers, they would've knocked before entering like polite beings. *I* knocked and entered properly. My wife has been very insistent I act like a somewhat civilized being and knock before entering. I do it to humor her and when I decide to just pop in, it's far more entertaining because they expect me to knock first."

"Who are you?"

"I'm the Devil, little girl. Shouldn't you be asking who you are? That's a better question. Who I am doesn't at all influence who you are, and who you are has changed compared to a few hours ago. I do love when angels do the heavy lifting, so I don't have to. I am not nearly as gentle and considerate as the asshole angels."

My mother, who matched my earliest memories, jumped on a purple-winged angel, bludgeoning his shoulders with a black purse. "Don't you touch my husband, you freak of an angel!"

"And that would be your grandfather," the Devil explained before he pointed at the other newcomers, all of whom had colored wings. "They are also more distant relatives, and while I appreciate that they contributed to the existence of my devil's bride, they live to annoy me."

"My mother seems to dislike him."

"She loves him to a shameful degree. Alas, he is a rather aggressive archangel. He does like to wade into battle and ask questions after. She's showing her love through wholesome violence. Don't kill each other. That would make things complicated and cultivating her seed for my devil would be troublesome. Do you know how hard it is to find an appropriate lineage for a seed's renewal?"

"No. I don't want to know. Don't tell me. And if my name isn't Layla, you can tell me, but if it's stupid, you'll just have to keep calling me Layla."

"You got the rather stereotypical Lilith, as you're the first demoness born of this era, and your species does like to lead men into temptation. You're not all that good at leading men to temptation, as you're disgustingly monogamous for a succubus. In that, you're a lot like my wife. I'm not good at sharing. Neither are you. Your father is also not very good at sharing. Your mother doesn't mind sharing, but your father keeps her amused. This sort of thing happens with my demons from time to time. Many are gloriously naughty, but every now and again, I'm given a corrupted seed. These corrupted seeds produce demonesses like you. But you corrupted a unicorn, so I'm quite pleased with you. You went for quality over quantity, and I can live with this."

Dean sighed.

Paul snickered and gave the unicorn a slap

on his rump. "Don't worry, Dean. He likes you. If he didn't, you'd already be a smear on the wall. The Devil does not like when anyone bothers his favored demons and devils. That's his angelic nature toying with him. He always enjoys when the underlings pull a fast one on one of the generals, and your father wiped that devil from existence, took the seed, and locked it in a box. He spends every morning dribbling holy water on the seed out of pure spite."

"I really should reclaim that seed, but my devil is having a good time, and I'd hate to ruin his fun. It's extended revenge, although he'll be a little less motivated in his daily torture sessions." The Devil laughed. "Who am I kidding? Your father will invite you to his home so you can have fun with the seed, too. You've my permission to gift the seed to your daughter should you want or keep it for yourself. The seed will be fully purified for your enjoyment."

"I'll leave that up to her," my father replied. "But thank you."

"Just be aware it's a devilish seed, and it should be replanted sooner than later. It's a little unbalancing with it just sitting around doing nothing."

My father held out his hand, and a small, black box appeared in his palm, which smoked and stank of sulfur. "Do you wish this child, Layla? You have choices. You can have the seed planted in a new life lost, you may choose to carry the seed to term more naturally, or you can choose not to have the seed at all. That devil has paid his dues for his crime, and a devilish child would be a challenge for you both. Devils do thrive in loving homes despite their nature. It would be a good way to cultivate more alliances between demons and devils, too." My father sighed. "You'll be a disgustingly doting mother, I'm sure. Your mother certainly is, and she's been giving me the eye."

"Says the disgustingly doting father," my mother said, still hard at work beating the archangel with her purse. "Don't fill her ears with lies. And don't you pretend you aren't planning on requesting a seed for another child. You've been sighing over that seed each morning, but you absolutely wouldn't."

"Because of me?"

"It's impossible to raise a child while knowing you were somewhere out there," my mother replied. She draped her chin over my —our—grandfather's shoulder. "He'll want time to settle, get to know you, and then have another child once you're safely settled with your stallion."

"The seed can wait. It exists, and that is sufficient to maintain the balance," the Devil said, his tail lashing side to side. "It's been a while since there's been an equine devil born. It would be the first of this age. I like it. Perhaps as your third or fourth born. He would be loved but not your heir, and that is for the best. I like surprises, and I'd like to see what surprises the heir of a demoness and a unicorn will become without any meddling."

I considered the problem of the devil who'd made a mess of my life, and after a few moments of thought, unlike my father, I couldn't bring myself to want revenge at all. Revenge changed nothing for me; it would not undo the circumstances of my life, and it seemed like a waste to me. My father had handled the matter, and I saw no need to add to the tragedy.

"You're a smart one," the Devil praised, reaching over and patting me on the head.

I snatched the nearest paintbrush, snapped the handle in half, and went for the Devil with the jagged edge. Before I could sink the splintered wood into his face, Paul wrapped his arm around me and held me back.

"Stop making everyone want to kill you," the angel complained.

"But it's fun, Paul. What will make someone snap? All I had to do was tell her she was smart, and she went right for my face. It's like there's a little violence switch, and if you say anything nice to her, her fuse blows and off she goes. Isn't she cute?"

Dean whipped his head around and bit the Devil hard enough to draw flaming blood, and since that wasn't enough to satisfy the stallion, he surged forward a stride, bucked.

The Devil crashed into me, and Paul lost his grip on my waist.

Before I could stab Satan, my father waded into the fray, took my paint brush, and gave me the box containing the precious seed. "Guard this until you figure out what you want to do with it. While the Devil loves a good brawl, let's not flatten the entire hotel, please."

The angels, for all they lacked heads, had one hell of a stare, which concentrated on my father.

"That's so creepy. How can beings without eyes do that? They're staring at you. They're really staring at you. I can feel it. I can't stab their eyes out to make them stop because they don't have any eyes!" Of all the things that'd happened, it amazed me I reached my limit coping with the headless angels.

My father smiled. "You'll get used to it eventually. Don't you worry about them; they're mostly harmless."

Epilogue: I wanted to paint the entire lot of them.

MY LIFE HAD CHANGED, and I wasn't sure what I thought about that.

In the days following Paul rummaging through my memories and helping me to discover the truth, I'd discovered the angel had done more than just add buffers to give me a chance to adapt to my new life and circumstances.

He'd done something, something that offered little nudges in the right direction when I didn't understand what I was supposed to do. The first of my obstacles involved displays of affection. Before Paul rummaging about in my head and making some key adjustments, I'd reacted with violence, reaching for the nearest item I could turn into a weapon.

A still, quiet voice reined in those instincts, buying me enough time to determine if I wanted to accept the offered affection.

It'd taken time, but I'd learned to accept Dean rubbing my feet, and he waited for when I was ready to handle more.

As such, he broke through those walls first.

We'd been watching a television show, although he paused it more often than not to explain the nuances of reality versus dramatic portrayals meant to entertain. The shows ate away time, but I'd learned a few important things: I liked Dean's voice, I loved his patience, and I enjoyed his company.

The longer I stayed with him, the more I recognized I'd fight to keep him.

Then, after watching my mother, the cues from that still, quiet voice made sense. She often pounced on my father or our angelic great-whatever grandfather seeking affection. Sometimes, she'd even target a member of Dean's family, although she left Dean alone.

He was mine, and I appreciated she recognized that.

Every time, her victim would feign surprise over her latest assault and fall prey to her. Once she'd subdued her target, she snuggled close and simply relished their company.

It had taken me a week of watching how others asked for or demanded attention before I'd decided to follow my mother's example.

Waiting for a moment when no one else was in the room, I pounced and drove him to the floor, snuggling him into submission. Making him laugh, as he'd done after figuring out who had pounced him and why, had rose to one of my top priorities.

I hadn't yet found the courage to seek affection from anyone else, but I planned to target my father next. He liked cuddling, even with angels, and accepted attention from anyone who would give it to him. After my father, I would target my mother, as she seemed like she would require more affection than my father before being satisfied. It bothered me I struggled when everyone else so readily sought and received attention from others.

Even the Devil liked being with people. Once, after a shopping trip with Xena to the art store, I'd returned to the hotel to a pile of angels, my parents, the Devil, and unicorns snuggled together watching television.

I'd taken a picture, as I doubted anyone would believe me if I told them what I'd witnessed without evidence.

Then, to help make certain I closed the doors of my past behind me for good, the unicorns took me out of the city, created a crystal grove in the middle of the forest, and staged a war meeting.

They wanted the blood of my former slavers, and they meant to turn it into paint. I'd vetoed that before anyone could get carried away. I didn't want to paint with blood. To keep me from murdering his stubborn family, Dean had promised to take me to a museum nearby, one that had an exhibit of my artwork. The herd fixated on their next scheme: returning all of my art to me, so I could decide what should become of my life's work.

My first trip to the museum ended with a deep sense of awe, that I'd somehow created something so beautiful while trapped in a cell, unaware I'd done nothing wrong to deserve my fate. Through my long and slow walk through the gallery, where I faced my memories, Dean stayed by my side.

Angels, devils, and demons alike kept claiming they loved me. The still, quiet, and guiding voice promised I only needed to look at Dean to understand it was possible for someone to love me, a flawed succubus with zero understanding of how to be a good succubus.

My second trip to the museum warned me of life to come. An over-enthusiastic herd of unicorns in their human forms dragged me through every exhibit, studying every last inch of the building preparing to test its security in the hopes of robbing the place blind.

I hadn't enjoyed that trip as much. My parents had kidnapped Dean, using him to make sure I attended our first family dinner.

In Hell.

With the Devil, his wife, and his spitfire cat of a daughter.

His daughter interested me, as she'd caught herself a stallion, too. Hers was a blue-gray tinged with green, and he liked showing off his teeth, which were meant for tearing through meat. He had a human form, too, and he seemed resigned to his fate when dealing with his father-in-law but so in love with his wife I wondered how I would change if I, too, could be capable of such an emotion.

I wanted to paint the entire lot of them and capture that love somehow, displaying it for the world to see.

The Devil, being the asshole ruler over all other assholes, had exposed my thoughts, resulting in a date to sketch and paint to my heart's content.

It'd been a rather cordial affair, and I'd learned my mother had waited my entire life for a chance to dress me up as a doll.

To my horror and dismay, I'd liked it. I'd even, under threat of death if she told a soul, tested patting her shoulder. As the display of affection hadn't killed me, I hugged her.

She'd hugged me back, and she'd rubbed my back like I'd seen people do on television. Afterwards, in the safety of my hotel room, in a gap when Dean and his sister had been stolen for a strategy session, I'd cried for everything I'd lost.

Until then, I hadn't known I could cry at all.

The third time, I had gone with my parents, who had treated my paintings as priceless treasures they wanted gracing their walls and their walls alone. Dean felt the same way.

In time, my parents would wage war with the unicorn, and I'd be stuck in the middle.

I looked forward to it.

Unfortunately for my parents, I planned to side with the damned unicorn. I'd somewhat adapted to having parents. I'd figured out how to handle hugging someone else without trying to stab them with improvised weapons.

I'd even won the museum curator's grudging respect, although we developed a love-hate relationship. He wanted to keep my art, but he didn't want to be haunted by devils, angels, the Devil, and a bunch of nosy, prissy and beautiful unicorns. If I let any of them have their way, I'd be the grand prize of their battle.

With the museum's blessings, the unicorns schemed and went to work. Either way, the paintings would be given to me. If the herd busted through the museum's security, the paintings would be paid for in labor, shoring up the building's defenses against people seeking priceless treasures. If we failed to rob the place, we'd buy them for a sum of ten million dollars.

I really hoped we succeeded at robbing the museum, as Paul's meddling helped me understand the value of such a number. Apparently, everyone thought I could earn as much or more with new paintings, too.

My artwork had traveled the world, and museums sought exhibits like the one we'd purchase from them.

Until my first visit, I hadn't known something as fascinating as museums could exist.

My life had changed, and I liked it.

ONE MONTH and two weeks after my fateful day in court, my misfit family, a herd of unicorns, a pack of angels, and the Devil converged several blocks away from the museum. I had no idea what I was doing with them, but I was dressed head to toe in a dark, matte material. Everyone else wore the same attire, and masks covered our faces, wrapped around our heads, and kept our hair from making an escape.

Hair, during a heist, created trouble. We'd spent an entire three days fighting over the issue of hair, its loss, and the problems hairs posed during an investigation. The first option, met with immediate refusals from the vain unicorns, involved a head-to-toe shave.

Under no circumstances could the beauty of a unicorn be blemished.

If I rolled my eyes any harder, I'd hurt myself.

"Why am I here?" I asked for the third time, not expecting an answer.

Everyone pointed at Dean.

"That's not an answer. It wasn't an answer the other two times you idiots pointed at him. You left me at the hotel to do your various scheming other times. Why am I here?"

My mother laughed, and the skin-tight outfit on her redefined scandalous. "You're here because there's something you need to see here. If you stayed at the hotel, all you'd see is a news report, which wouldn't be anywhere as nice as witnessing it for yourself. Relax, darling. Everything will be fine. This is going to be a cakewalk."

"Why is it going to be a cakewalk? Cakewalks are a lie. I have not yet seen a cakewalk end in cake. Why do you insist on lying to me? Not a single one of your cakewalks has resulted in cake. If you could stop being evasive, I would really appreciate it."

"Call me Mom or Mother, and I will spill the Devil's secrets."

"Hey," the Devil protested. "That's not nice."

"I'm a demon. One of your demons, specifically. Since when was being nice a part of my job description?"

The Devil lashed his tail but kept quiet. His wife's presence, who also went out of her way to redefine scandalous, had something to do with that.

"She has you there," the Devil's wife, the true controller of the many hells and its fiery lord, muttered. She muttered in such a way everyone could hear her without issue and made it clear the Devil had lost yet again.

"I see how it is. Once succubi get together, they live to create trouble for me. Next, you two are going to join forces and try to take over the Earth." The Devil's tail stilled, and he stood taller. "Please do, actually. I'd enjoy watching that. Would a little begging help to encourage you ladies?"

Xena snorted. "We've been over this before. I'm taking over the Earth, but I could use some good henchwomen. I'll take good care of them and return them in similar condition."

Dean and the rest of the unicorns replied, "No."

"Why are you so mean to me?" Xena complained.

"Focus," I ordered. "Someone please coherently explain why I am here and not sleeping. I had plans to steal Dean's blankets tonight. Mine are not warm enough."

Dean laughed. "If you want to snuggle, all you have to do is pounce or ask. Dragging is also acceptable, as is waggling your finger in invitation. You can even join me on the couch at your whim and take over my lap. I'm easy."

The unicorn would finish driving me crazier within a week, I'd enjoy it, and I'd make sure I got him and his blanket when I conquered his person. "Focus, Dean. Focus. And for fuck's sake, someone please tell me why I'm here."

The Devil snickered, and he gestured in the direction of the museum. "In twenty or so minutes, men in vans will come to the museum and attempt to either retrieve or recover your paintings to make evidence of their wrongdoing disappear. We are going to trip the alarm systems as they enter, bar their escape, and prevent them from accessing the exhibit with your paintings. While the police are occupied, we will take advantage of the gap in security to take the paintings. This will uphold our promise to test the museum's security system, and it'll allow the unicorns to do what they do best. Protectorate species are so troublesome like that. Those behind the art ring will be arrested for attempted theft, where it will be revealed that the paintings were created through unpaid child labor, which then led to your wrongful confinement as an adult. As you're a succubus, you would have counted as a child for the first fifty years of your life. The paintings, which will be in our custody per our agreement with the museum, will be lawfully signed over to you. The museum will be compensated in funds claimed from the defendants because it was sold illegal artwork and had no realistic way of knowing the artwork was illegally acquired. After that is settled, you will be able to loan the paintings to museums as exhibits, even including newer pieces you paint as you please. The museum will gain prestige, as it will be able to do a gallery greeting with you, the artist, present for the reveal of the reopened exhibit. This benefits everyone, and you'll be properly paid for your work."

I narrowed my eyes and considered how best I could trample, murder, or otherwise mutilate those who'd caused so much suffering. "How many of the art ring will be here?"

"Most of them will be in attendance. They're very determined to retrieve your paintings. There's a reason for that. They used stolen works as the foundation for some of your paintings, and this will help draw other parties into the case." The Devil rubbed his hands together. "Come along, come along. We have a schedule. It wouldn't do to be late."

The angels, who wore similar attire and had covered their wings with a black, gauzy material, headed for the museum. Without being able to see their wings and the colorful bands on their feathers, I couldn't tell who was who. They'd even gone so far as to change their voices to be neutral and lifeless.

Sneaky angels.

"What do you have to say about this?" I asked them, deciding the angels were the safest of my options. Dean, being Dean, stayed close to me.

"I would say it is unfair to abuse our powers in such a fashion, little granddaughter, but *He* allows it, for *He* hates when we whine too much about the injustices done to our offspring. Honestly, I'll enjoy it. There will be a rather sad and bloody accident in the museum as a certain would-be thief impales himself on my sword while running through the halls. It will be a tragedy."

My grandfather's eagerness for the kill reminded me angels were not at all like the stories portrayed. Then again, the stories had neglected to mention they lacked heads.

I could only think of one thing to ask my violence-loving grandfather. "And your general enjoyment of permissible violence has nothing to do with this?"

"You have become a sadly responsible and gentle being. Paul, I will beat you for adjusting my granddaughter inappropriately."

The angel laughed. "I didn't adjust her inappropriately. I merely coached her on social behaviors she had no opportunity to learn. She is much happier now that she can pounce her stallion without fear of retribution. I'm sure she'll start seeking you for affection soon enough. My workings were designed to help develop her partnership with her unicorn as a priority. She's progressing nicely. As she becomes more comfortable with physical interaction, she will seek it more. I'm sure you'll have your turn soon."

For fuck's sake. "Would a hug make you insufferable, hug-happy beings happy?"

"Yes," everyone chorused.

"I will pay out one hug to all participants if this is finished sooner than later, please and thank you. Also, should you take the heads of those who came up with this plan, I do not want them delivered to me on a platter. I don't want to see any decapitated heads at all. Keep your murder and mayhem to yourself."

The Devil, the host of angels, and my father disappeared with a bang loud enough to make my ears ring. Unlike every other time I'd seen someone teleport, there were no lights or stench of brimstone.

My mother laughed. "Now you've done it and the rest of us will just have to sit here and wait for the end results. How boring."

I didn't want exciting. I didn't even want the thrill of testing the museum's alarm system. I wanted the past to finish dying already so it would leave me alone. "I like efficiency."

"Well, you certainly got it with that offer. That lot has been after a hug since they heard you'd started giving them to your stallion. No is an allowed answer, and you never told them when you would pay out your hug. Choose a time that you prefer. If they had wanted a hug on a schedule, they would have done a better job of demanding terms."

I considered that. "You make a good point. I didn't tell them when. I just said if they finished this sooner than later, I would, at some point in the future, hug them. I will do that. Eventually. I will be a good daughter for the first time in my life, and I will hug you first to make them jealous."

"That's my girl. We'll make a proper de-moness out of you yet. Just make sure you keep giving your stallion affection. They require it from time to time. Also, you're a good daughter. You may not realize it yet, but you are. It helps you're a succubus. You can get away with murder and still be a good daughter. I'm concerned there's a cat in your heritage I don't know about, however. You are far too fond of warm things."

Dean nudged me with his elbow. "You do like sleeping in warm places, rather like a cat. I'm available for any warmings of your person you require. You should listen to your mother, lovely lady that she is."

"Save your attempted seductions of my daughter for a better time," my mother ordered. "We don't have all night for her to work her nerves out on you, and there are no suitable places nearby. Really. You're as bad as an incubus most of the time, Dean. She's not going to escape you. She gets her monogamous tendencies from my side of the family, alas."

"Thank you for having such a wonderful daughter."

"You're welcome. Do try to bring her home from time to time. If you can return her a little more eager for affection, it would be appreciated."

"She's already learned she can manipulate

an entire host of angels, the Devil, and a devilish general through the power of displayed affection. I think she'll be fine. She'll have an entire herd to practice on."

Dean's mother and father, as mismatched as all their children, waved from the midst of the gathered unicorns.

It was then, surrounded by those who'd become the rest of my life, I realized several important truths.

I didn't need any of my old art. I could paint new, better, and happier things.

I didn't need revenge. I'd already gotten it in the form of freedom and a chance at a happy life.

I didn't need anything to change. Everything had changed from the moment Dean had trotted into my life in a North Carolina courthouse.

I didn't need a family. I already had one, although I had a lot left to learn about being part of that family.

I didn't need anything other than what I already had.

"We should go get some cupcakes," I announced. "Museum robberies are overrated. Have the Devil take the paintings. It's not like an alarm system can defy the forces of good, evil, or whatever they are. Cupcakes are so much better than heists."

Dean laughed. "You're something else, Layla."

Yes, I was, and I liked it.

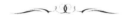

Thanks for reading!

The next book in the series is Grave Humor, which releases on May 12, 2020 at all major retailers.

About R.J. Blain

Want to hear from the author when a new book releases? You can sign up at her website (thesneakykittycritic.com). Please note this newsletter is operated by the Furred & Frond Management. Expect to be sassed by a cat. (With guest features of other animals, including dogs.)

A complete list of books written by RJ and her various pen names is available at https://books2read.com/rl/The-Fantasy-Worlds-of-RJ-Blain.

RJ BLAIN suffers from a Moleskine journal obsession, a pen fixation, and a terrible tendency to pun without warning.

When she isn't playing pretend, she likes to think she's a cartographer and a sumi-e painter.

In her spare time, she daydreams about being

a spy. Should that fail, her contingency plan involves tying her best of enemies to spinning wheels and quoting James Bond villains until she is satisfied.

RJ also writes as Susan Copperfield and Bernadette Franklin. Visit RJ and her pets (the Management) at thesneakykittycritic.com.

FOLLOW RJ & HER ALTER EGOS ON BOOKBUB:
RJ BLAIN
SUSAN COPPERFIELD
BERNADETTE FRANKLIN